Edition
„ H y p e r l i n k "

3

Original title
Vladimir Pištalo
MILENIJUM U BEOGRADU

Република Србија
МИНИСТАРСТВО КУЛТУРЕ И ИНФОРМИСАЊА

Овај пројекат је подржало Министарство културе
и информисања Републике Србије.
This project was funded by Ministry of Culture and
Information Republic of Serbia.

VLADIMIR PIŠTALO

MILLENNIUM IN BELGRADE

A novel

Translation from Serbian into English:
Bogdan Rakić and John Jeffries

ΑΓΩΡΑ

For Mirjana Živković

PROLOGUE

A legend about the founding of Belgrade tells a story of a man who insulted the centaurs that lived around the slopes of Avala since the beginning of time. The ground shook under the angry hooves of the centaurs. Their screams rent the sky. The man escaped by the skin of his teeth as he dove into the river. He heard the hiss of arrows that pelted the surface of the water. The centaurs stopped at the bank, neighed, and pawed at the mud. The fugitive bobbed up in the middle of the Sava and caught his breath. He choked down a lot of water before he reached the other side. Exhausted, he collapsed under the Kalemegdan cliff, at the spot where the Sava and the Danube meet, and closed his eyes.

He dreamed of a city.

He dreamed of temples and palaces. He dreamed of theaters surrounding the square where poets recited verses. He dreamed of well-dressed old men and women, full of life, who were strolling through parks. He dreamed of lovers who intoxicated each other with their breath. He dreamed of sculptures that dotted the squares and the facades of buildings. He dreamed of a thousand restaurants which served the food of a thousand nations. He dreamed of wine-shops organized as neatly as libraries. He dreamed of a city with two rivers that washed its worries away and left it carefree.

He dreamed of bookstores and tea-shops where a man could comfortably grow old. He dreamed of a town where it was a pleasure to experience the change of seasons. He dreamed of a place that seduced him with details and made him fall in love with the whole. He dreamed of the City. That was a city of eternal noon, without twilight and shadows. Angels strolled through the streets, and from windows women showered them with confetti from pillow-cases. White arms waived to the dreamer from balconies.

When the man opened his eyes, an angel was standing above him. The angel had eyes the man had never seen before. The angel pointed his finger at the cliff above the waters and said:

"Look!"

The man looked along the angel's finger and – everything was there! There was a city on the cliff. The walls, whiter than a cuttlebone, gleamed in the sun. Clusters of architecture rose on top of each other in charming disarray.

This was long before I was born in Belgrade, met Irina and fell in love with her there. And yet, I write about this as an eye-witness. That's possible because it all happened in Dreamtime, which precedes, follows, and intertwines with time. It all happened in Sacred Spring, in eternity, in every-time-and-place time. That's why I can testify how delighted the dreamer was to see the walls which would finally shield him from the howling wilderness.

With horror in his eyes, the dreamer drank in his dream--come-true. He only had to open its gates and settle down in it. Suddenly he felt too small to accept responsibility for his dream. He wanted to shriek. He wanted to scream. He wanted to hide his head under his wing. Now that his dream came true, he could burst like a soap bubble. The dreamer's lip twisted, and he scoffed at himself and what he wanted the most. On his mushy legs, he took the first step backwards. Then he made the second one and the third one. At the moment he turned his back on the city for good, the angel's scream boomed from the ramparts of chalk. Without looking back, the dreamer left the unfinished dream and returned to the howling wilderness.

The gods who granted the man's wish, placed a horrible curse on the city:

Let this place be a wound. As soon as a scab covers it, let dirty nails rip it away. Let generations of sons never continue what generations of fathers began. Let the people in this city always scoff at what they want the most.

And that was the gods' punishment for the man who turned his back on his dream.

CHAPTER 1

On the emperor's funeral and the enlightened discussion
we had on this occasion

Ba-bump, ba-bump, ba-bump...

On its main channel, Radio Belgrade broadcasted the heartbeat of Yugoslavia's Marshal, Josip Broz Tito. When silence settled, Bane told me:

"The sound of history."

On that day, May 4, 1980, in a special edition, daily *Politika* conceded:

"The great heart fell silent. Our president, Marshal Josip Broz Tito, is dead."

The headline sobbed:

"Dark anguish and deep sorrow engulf the working class, all peoples and ethnic groups of our nation, every single individual, industrial worker, soldier, farmer, each and every artist, member of Communist Youth and teenager, young girl and mother."

At the soccer game between Hajduk and Red Star, in the forty-third minute of the first half, the ball stopped rolling and tears started falling.

A seven day period of mourning was decreed.

Newspapers launched a three day campaign of orgasmic lamentation. The Marshal was buried on my birthday, four days after the official day of his death. Boris, Bane, Zora and Irina were in my apartment. We drank some Slovenian Laški riesling and watched the broadcast of the funeral. We turned the sound off and played Knopfler's "Sultans of Swing" five times in a row.

When we were schoolboys, Boris was my stand-in in fights. His face exuded quiet masculinity. He could open a beer bottle with his teeth.

"What's in the paper?" he asked.

I didn't know, but Bane did. He recited the headlines in a voice of a petty thief declaring his innocence.

"From the UN podium, for more than three hours, representatives from Africa, Asia, Eastern and Western Europe, Latin America, the Southeast Asia Treaty Organization, the Arab League, and non-aligned countries paid their respects to our deceased president. Seven hundred reporters from forty-four countries enabled 1.5 billion people to follow the funeral. Tito was a person who belonged to everyone, so his death is a loss to all progressive people in the world." As he reeled off this litany, Bane was trying to catch a star with his left hand and keep his heart from jumping out of his chest with his right. His voice broke, and he wiped off a fake tear... "He was... He was... He was the architect of the Non-aligned Movement."

All this was happening at the point where the gorgeous Irina wasn't Boris' girlfriend anymore, and way before she became mine.

"Be quiet, let's really pay attention," Irina said and turned up the volume.

The TV taught me that – as a Yugoslav in mourning – I should find some consolation in the fact that the funeral was attended by a number of foreign statesmen with whom the deceased President hunted drugged bears in the forests of the Socialist Federal Republic of Yugoslavia. The Swedish, Belgian, and Norwegian kings arrived in Belgrade. Sandro Pertini represented Italy, Leonid Brezhnev – the Soviet Union, Margaret Thatcher – Great Britain, Walter Mondale – the US, Francois Mitterrand – France, Willi Brandt – Germany, Indira Gandhi – India, Kenneth Kaunda –

Zambia, and Hua Guofeng – China. Prince Henrik of Denmark, the Duke of Edinburgh, the Nepalese Prince Gyanendra, and Holland's princes Claus and Bernhard were also there. The Secretary General of the UN Kurt Waldheim's arrival was confirmed.

"It's good he's coming too," Boris said simplemindedly.

The TV told us that the representatives of UNESCO, the Arab League, the European Parliament, and the European Council arrived in Belgrade as well.

"How nice."

President Jimmy Carter's mother Liliane set her trembling foot on the Belgrade airport's runaway. With an uneasy smile, Vice-President Walter Mondale assisted her. A state of mourning was declared in fifty-three countries.

"That's exactly what our megalomania feeds on," Zora said without taking her eyes from the TV. "The high that we enjoy so much now will equal the crash we'll inevitably experience later."

"Play that record again!" Boris demanded.

"No. Shut up!" retorted Zora tersely.

"Zora, please open me another bottle from that cache over there."

Zora gave me a long look.

The TV spewed information like a gutter in a downpour.

It was so comforting to know that:

1) the divided world put their flags at half-mast and came together in praise of Tito

2) everywhere he went, Tito was met with smiles and seen off with tears

3) the fall of the majestic oak that was rooted in the hearts of working men shattered the world

4) millions of people sympathized with all the peoples of Yugoslavia.

Bane blew a wisp of hair that fell over his eye. His girlfriend Marija ditched him on the day of Tito's death. She was the vocalist and saxophone player in his band *Acoustic Shadow*. He played with them for a year. By the way, the name was based on the fact that the sound of a battle is better heard from a distance than from up close, where it's within the "acoustic shadow." Bane worked hard at getting drunk.

Smacking his lips he asked, "I wonder what all the peoples of Yugoslavia are doing right now?"

Zora said:

"I read and I remembered. Slovenes carry out their assigned duties with aching hearts. Croats have lost a part of themselves. Bosnians suffer from true human sorrow. In Vojvodina, people cry: Tito's accomplishments will live on! Montenegrins are dignified in their pain. Macedonian hearts speak eloquently. Krajina is frozen in its stoic, masculine grief. The Srem lowlands are flooded with the tears of anguished farmers."

"Bane's music is dead," Bane said.

"My mother doesn't care about music," Zora shouted. "My mother cares about Tito. She's in tears."

It was my birthday, a benchmark in a life I didn't understand, and I listened to the TV's summary of important events. On a special train, Tito's body arrived from Ljubljana to Belgrade. In a closed casket, the body lay in state in the Yugoslav Assembly Building. Struggling with sorrow, two hundred World War II heroes wore their medals of valor in the procession around the bier. One in five Yugoslavs passed by that bier in the next couple of days.

I liked that the city was brightly lit all night. And it was… wondrous! People waited in endless lines to bow their heads before the dead Tito.

"Look at those lines," I told Bane as we were standing under the shadows of the row of trees across the street from the Assembly Building, in the brightly lit city full of muted people. "Right now, the heart of this city is a corpse."

"I like it a lot," he said. "This is unreal. As if this kind of Belgrade was painted by Paul Delvaux and the funereal ceremonies directed by Luis Bunuel."

In the Surrealist Belgrade, the newcomers waited all day to pass by Tito's bier and pay their last respects. The silent columns of people snaked all the way from Zeleni Venac Market to the Assembly Building. Green uniforms with red crosses distributed drinking water at the Terazije and Skadarlija daycare centers. The centers were staffed by physicians in case some visitors fainted. Newspapers reported that policemen – whom they referred to as "hardened law enforcement veterans" – let pedestrians jay-walk because those "different pedestrians" were in a hurry to join the procession. It was clearly implied that the Yugoslav cops treated them with kid gloves...

It was interesting to observe these "columns of pain and silence" live. Truly, the representatives of Yugoslavia's various ethnic groups gathered in front of the Assembly Building, stood in lines, and passed out in the heat. In the words of a witty reporter, everyone "turned into an ear and a tear." Another inspired reporter noticed that in Belgrade "everyone stood still – only the rivers flowed."

Boris poured himself a glass of Slovenian Laški riesling, put down the bottle, and scratched behind his ear:

"I'd like to know what kind of person Tito really was."

Soggy with tears, the newspapers had the answer. It was put forth like this:

"Tito was a uniquely humane individual. All his battles were fought for the common man! This is the only battle he lost! Tito was a symbol of a generation! His accomplishments fill us with pride and require us to answer the call of duty! His contribution to science is invaluable! He was great in small matters! He took care of chess and chess players! However, the great ones never leave this world. That's why our pain is so motivating."

"Motivating for what?" Boris asked from the corner of his mouth.

Bane saw the use of the glass as an unnecessary convention. He was drinking from the bottle. He started to call out:

"I-riii-naaa!"

The gorgeous Irina didn't respond.

"I-riii-naaa!"

"What?"

"When was the first time you wanted to get laid?"

Irina didn't say anything. While Bane waited for her answer to this trivial question, the TV addressed the essential issue regarding human mortality and the transience of this world:

"In Belgrade's main department store, the items that sell almost exclusively are mourning attire and badges with Tito's image," the TV said. "The author Tone Svetina told us how Tito's generosity became apparent when he was hunting." We also learned that "the names of all our victories will be engraved on Tito's tomb."

"I-riii-naaa!"

Like every average Yugoslav, Irina watched the funeral ceremony with moved boredom, so she naturally failed to respond to Bane's drunken call.

"C'mon, don't push it," Boris warned Bane.

"And when did you start jerking off?" Bane asked in a serious voice.

At that moment, the TV reached a crescendo and the anchor's voice cracked into a falsetto: "Tito outdid his epoch! He's the most eminent person in history! Bravo! The greatest humanist! May he live long! The greatest man in our history died..."

"Being thirteen years of age," Boris retorted. "What other age could it be?"

The deadly serious female anchor didn't pay any attention to our trivial conversation. She pedantically stated that statesmen from one hundred and twenty one nations, who represented three billion and seven hundred million people, attended Tito's funeral.

"How many times a day?" Bane wouldn't leave it alone.

Boris scratched his short red hair.

"About five. I wanted to do it more often, but didn't have time."

"Well, that's exactly what the problem is," Zora cut in. "The problem is that all Yugoslavs share the pharaoh-like megalomania of their own president. We must see the world in superlatives."

"Why did these people come to Belgrade?" the TV asked and immediately offered an answer to its own rhetorical question. "From all over the world, they came in order to bow before Tito, one of the greatest individuals of our time... The universal man... This funeral is a world summit in itself. Centuries will not obscure Tito's work... His death is the sole battle he lost!" the TV prattled on. "Nothing like this has ever happened in the history of the world!"

Out of breath, one man confessed on the screen:

"What I felt as I passed by his bier is something I'll recount to my kids and to my grandkids..."

"We keep on working, you know, but it ain't the same, you know, it's never been this way," a factory worker was searching for words. "I ain't ashamed to cry, you know."

"Fuck you, apes," the drunken Bane cussed. "Fuck you in the ass. The whole world."

I loved and respected the world. I believed in Durkheim's idea that society possesses all the attributes of God. Since humankind was the largest society in the world, the United Nations to me was – God.

"This is the end of our era of Enlightened Absolutism," Bane noted.

"What's to come after it? Endarkened Absolutism?" I snorted, pleased with my own joke. However, as soon as I shut my mouth, I realized that it was the end of an epoch. A chill came down from the stars and wrapped around me like a shroud. I asked in a changed voice:

"What will happen now?"

"The plague will come," Zora said. "Only tales will remain. Like in *The Decameron*."

Irina came up to me from behind, pressed her lips against my cheek and said:

"Happy coming of age and happy birthday!"

CHAPTER 2

Transformation

Belgrade rock-'n-roll was never as good as it was after the death of Josip Broz Tito. With his eternal love and hate for Marija, my friend Bane Janović kept putting together New Wave bands like *Acoustic Shadow, Youthful but Fat, Crippled with Fear,* and *Kafka's Fiancés.*

With the advent of New Wave, such energy was unleashed on Belgrade that even its statues were startled. A lot of excited chatter spilled out into the streets. There was a spark in every eye. I could say: This is mine. This city is finally mine. This is something from my world.

It all started when Bane Janović found a medal of valor from World War II. He flicked his Zippo lighter open and heated the needle. He pinched his breast and pinned the medal through his skin. He ground his teeth and said: Let's go! Bane succinctly defined his music thus:

1) I'm desperate.
2) I have no girlfriend.
3) I can't play music.
4) There are many who can, but they have nothing to say.
5) I have something to say, but I don't know how.

Until they learned how to play, Bane and Marija recited texts from a primary reader, accompanied by a drum machine. They embraced the Zenith *avant-garde* movement from the twenties, parodied Socialist Realism and pop songs from the sixties. *Crippled with Fear* fell apart just before they were about to record an album. The best keyboard player in town left the group in order to dedicate himself to black magic. They had to phone a friend in Zagreb to cancel a gig at the Kulušić Club. When *Kafka's Fiancés* became a fixture on the scene, Bane started to mug for photographs in *Jukebox Magazine.*

"There's a dearth of reality in our town," he stated in an interview.

"I can't stand other people," he said in another one. "Because they are *the Other*, and anyway – why should I…"

"Do you consider yourself famous?" they asked him.

"I am famous when I'm happy," he responded in the words of Ian Dury.

On a May evening in 1982, *Kafka's Fiancés* played in a little squat castle-like building which once was called the Officers' Club. Seventy-nine years before, Dragutin Dimitrijević Apis and his co-conspirators left that same building on their way to assassinate the Serbian King Aleksandar Obrenović and his wife Draga Mašin. *Kafka's Fiancés* tore it up at the very place where, at one point, the members of the Black Hand organization pledged their vows. Whenever I think about Bane and Marija, I remember the name of their first album: *How Many of Them Do We Have and What?*

The *Kafka's Fiancés* bassist's hand reminded me of a paw of a dog scratching itself. In the cloud of stage fog, the drummer was barely able to pound his kit. Wearing a jacket with padded shoulders, Bane looked like Frankenstein. He was standing in the circle of a spotlight. He straightened up and threw off his jacket. The medal of valor from World War II shone on his bare chest. The fans were a huge dancing faceless body. They were a black Quasimodo. They responded to Bane with screams of encouragement.

What I witnessed looked like a mixture of macumba and a nineteenth century Neapolitan opera. The stage became a magical site of transformation. The soles of our feet tingled from the powerful loudspeakers. The bass shook our kidneys.

In the circle of spotlight, Bane started to twitch his shoulders. He moved his feet more from nervousness than from the music. I sensed he was struggling for control over his body and was slowly gaining it. At one point he broke the shackles of stage fright and barked into the mic. He started to dance in powerful disjointed movements. The fans went wild. Bane Janović, who had been barely able to manage his own body a moment before, now danced through the bodies of everyone in the audience.

It occurred to me that this was what Belgrade New Wave was all about – gaining control over oneself. I'd never seen Bane so serious in my entire life. He was the Indian chief Crazy Horse. He was a dervish in a swirling trance. Bane held the mic with both hands and kept the beat with his foot. I felt pride and envy. He dared to do what I had never dared to do. He dared to be himself. On the stage, Bane turned into a fire walker. He became a prophet who opens the skies with his gaze and the springs with his heels. Behind him, smoke billowed. The most beautiful and frightening thing in this world billowed through him. As I watched him at the concert, I realized that all the institutions of this world are merely security fences built around *charisma*. That prophetic power can turn a desert into an oasis, heal the crippled, wake the sleeping, fill eyes with tears…

The floodlights changed, and Bane's color changed. Now he was green like the spirit of peyote. Was that the man I grew up with? Shivers went down my spine when Marija stepped on the stage with her saxophone. She too was transformed.

Bane looked tragically serious. His bosom with the medal of valor swelled with pride. Sweat ran down his temples. He quit singing and looked only at Marija. She raised the saxophone and blew. It sounded like Behemoth's whistle in *The Master and*

Margarita. She blew and raised tempestuous winds. She blew and the curtains ruffled. She blew into the sails of our souls. A great wind lifted us. Marija bent backwards like a pilot of a sailboat and lifted us with her saxophone. The concert hall of dancing bodies turned into the *Flying Dutchman.* Marija blew into its sails and the ship flew above the city and the world. We all believed that we would all fly into space inhabited with iridescent, searing jelly fish, genies and the spirits of peyote.

CHAPTER 3

A portrait of Zora with *Oration on the Dignity of Man*

When Zora Stefanović and I were babies in the Belgrade Maternity Ward, the Fates decreed: These two will be friends. From the very beginning, I found her extremely likable and that has never changed. I knew how she was when she was a little girl. I knew all her fears and I loved the whole package.

"My father died when I was seven," she told me once. "That's when the whole world eclipsed and has never fully recovered."

After her father's death, a woman began to visit her in her dreams: at times she appeared as a little girl, at others as an old lady. She always wanted to come close to Zora and touch her. The woman drank the life out of her. Zora would wake up weakened. On the fifth anniversary of her father's death, the vampire appeared wearing a ballroom dress. She hid her teeth as she smiled. She eyed Zora with a horrible, fawning gaze and approached her on all fours. At that point, Zora's father entered the dream, stood between his daughter and the vampire, and shouted:

"Leave her alone!"

The fawning monster turned around, left the room, and never came back, but Zora's nightmares didn't end. Since then, she started to dream about her father every night. Zora's grandmother took her to her father's grave. She ordered her to lay a daisy across it and offer him a symbolic trade:

"I'll give you the white flower, you release me from your tower."

The nightmares ceased after that.

When Zora began to turn into a woman, her mother told her that she was plain, "so that she wouldn't become vain." Her mother loved to mention how many people – ha, ha – thought the two of them were sisters. In her own house, Zora grew up like Cinderella. I'm pretty sure she's never had a boyfriend nor has ever been kissed.

My friend Zora's eyes were stolen from a more beautiful face, from a more beautiful world. When the sky was cloudy, she became grey-eyed, like Athena. When she was angry, her eyes turned into green bottle flies in the August sun. All of us loved to read, but no one as much as Zora. She was the philosopher of our group.

When Boris Petrović defeated Joško Varežina and won the junior judo nationals, Zora told him that she couldn't understand why a man would put so much effort into learning how to beat up other people. Boris hugged her and yelled:

"Don't anyone dare touch her – she's my sister!"

When Bane Janović claimed in an interview that there was "a dearth of reality in our town," Zora flared up:

"You can't have any reality without investing in it!"

Bane got angry:

"Zora, you'll spend your life either being a smart ass or taking care of those who are better off than you."

"Thank God there's people like Zora," I took her side. "What would life be without good people like her? That would be no life at all…"

Zora considered all women with large breasts "vulgar" – except Irina Bojović. When these two got together, they talked about the world's hottest guys and the world's hottest pastries and giggled like little girls.

An ordinary person like myself is not meant to know a lot of people. The four friends I'm talking about were the four pillars of my universe. The chronicle of my city and my own chronicle rest on them. It turned out the Fates sent us down very different paths. I became a historian. Irina acquired a degree in architecture but never used it. Bane remained a ladies' man and musician. Boris became a judo champion and evolved into a, let's say, businessman. Zora – who as a little girl used to sing "Mama, give me matches and little gasoline to burn down the school and stay warm and clean" – became an assistant professor at the School of Applied Arts in Belgrade.

Zora was the most cosmopolitan person I knew even though she never traveled. She always wanted to see Gaudi's Barcelona and the Grand Canyon. She never saw them. Zora's commendable love of all things foreign sometimes resembled self-hatred.

"Not before I was eighteen did I realize I lived in Yugoslavia," she told me once. "I suppose, I've been living here as a punishment for what I did in my past life."

I looked down and said:

"We shouldn't be ashamed of who we are."

Zora responded:

"Nor should we accept the mold that circumstances pressed upon us." She quickly got up, fetched Pico della Mirandola's *Oration on the Dignity of Man*, and read the passage in which God addresses Man:

"Adam, I am not giving thee a permanent shelter, a shape that is thine only, or a unique function, so that thou canst – in accordance with thy own reasoning and desires – find a shape, function, and dwelling of thy own choosing... Other creatures' limitations art fixed in accordance with my Law, while thou art given the freedom to set thy own limitations. I placed thee in the center of the world, so that thou canst easily see everything there is in it. I made thee neither heavenly nor earthly, neither immortal nor mortal. I made thee so that, with honor and free will, thou canst sculpt thyself into any shape thou desire... Thou wilt be able to degenerate into lower, bestial life forms. In accordance with thy soul's judgement, thou wilt have the power to resurrect in higher, divine forms."

I often think of her who introduced this passage to me. Now I believe that she must have been religious. Where are you now, my Zora? You were always clearheaded and well-meaning. You always felt shame for those who were shameless. Largely, this chronicle is about you. This is a chronicle about all things beautiful that have only been ventured but never gained.

CHAPTER 4

On a man who never hesitated to quarrel with other people

Zora gave Boris a look and giggled.

"You know, you look dangerous."

"Of course I do," agreed Boris.

Zora cautiously touched our friend's shoulder.

"I mean, you *really* look dangerous."

"Of course! And do you know why?" exclaimed Boris. "Because I *am* a dangerous man!"

Boris looked exactly the way Xenophon described the Thracians: red-haired, freckled, with the eyes of a goat. He smiled the delicate smile of a wine taster. He looked nothing like the villain from a puppet show who rushes out on stage and growls:

"Grrr! I'm bad, I'm sooo bad."

I remembered one afternoon when Boris and I skipped school. We smoked *Filter 57* and spat on the ground in Tašmajdan Park. On the bench next to ours, some freckled Hans was sitting with his girlfriend. A man couldn't look at another human being more scornfully than Hans looked at me that afternoon. I passed by his bench with a small derisive grin. Hans believed that I had to endure his scornful smile while he didn't have to endure mine, and that was a problem.

"What's so funny?" he asked.

That was quite a bold remark considering that there were two of us. I didn't respond; I just clutched a volume containing two novels by Knut Hamsun, *Hunger* and *Pan*. It was as heavy as a brick.

Hans approached me from behind and asked again:

"What's so funny?"

Without a word, I turned around and smacked him across the face with Knut Hamsun. I hoped this inspired Dositej Obradović, the father of Serbian Enlightenment, to exclaim in heaven:

"Turn to books, brothers, to books – not to church bells and chimes!"

Hans was flabbergasted. To this day, I don't know what in the name of God he expected me to do. We grabbed each other by the throat. For a while, Boris watched as we grunted and struggled. Then he stepped in and laid two quick jabs into my opponent. Bye-bye Hans! I'll never forget this act of kindness. I'll also never forget Hans' girlfriend as she screamed:

"Let him go, you murderers!"

Zora always tried to convince us that man wasn't the product of his environment but of what he unites with within his heart. Boris believed in something quite the opposite:

"We're defined by who we are and who our family is," he lectured. "My brother is an idiot, and you're my friend. But, if you asked me to loan you ten grand, you wouldn't get it, while he would get it – as a gift."

Boris' father came from southern Serbia, from a place called Hicktown, while his mother was from neighboring Boonieville. People picked on Boris a lot because of his parents' background. The perception that, in a rural country like Yugoslavia, it was embarrassing to have farmers for relatives offers a perfect example of a distorted self-image and shame one feels looking into the mirror. Boris' classmates taunted him all the time about his "fuuuckin' aaaaccent" even though he didn't have any. But after he joined a judo club, the harassment tapered off. When Boris beat Joško Varežina and became the national junior champion, the guys forgot they had ever picked on him. His club later produced policemen and mobsters in equal measures. At tournaments, Boris became inseparable with his future bosom buddy Double Hulk.

Boris' father was a sergeant major. Even though he probably harassed the conscripts with "duck-and-cover" at boot camp, he was quite a decent fellow at home. The mother was a home maker. From the first day of their married life, Boris' parents saved with the goal of building the largest house in Hicktown. They resembled peasants who came to the city looking for work. They worked their butts off in order to earn the future jealousy of their fellow villagers. They were tightfisted and deprived themselves of everything in the name of that future jealousy. The mother reused frying oil all the time. The father walked around their apartment turning lights off. When they married, they lived so frugally they almost starved themselves. For dinner, they would stop in front of a restaurant and smell their fill of roasted meat. They believed that their house, once they build it, would become a meeting place for the large family they remembered from their childhood. Scattered all over Germany, Sweden, and the former Yugoslavia, that family would never come together.

Boris huffed and complained that his father was too "honest" as if honesty was a deadly disease. His father never missed a day of work even when he had a high fever. His mother was good looking in her youth. Whenever I went to visit them, I heard Aunty Maca muttering to herself in the kitchen as she made stuffed cabbage rolls:

"I really like being a woman, so I can be fickle like those ladies in the opera."

Boris' father would sit me next to him and shout:

"Maca, two coffees over here, pronto!"

"Smooth or bitter?" Aunty Maca asked from the kitchen.

"A little on the bitter side – like us hard workers drink."

Laughing, Boris told me how his father wooed his mother. One summer night, he walked by Maca's side as he usually did. Then he suddenly stopped and pointed his finger at the sky. He joyfully exclaimed:

"See that star?"

He then grabbed Maca by both shoulders and enthusiastically yelled:

"You're just like that star!"

"Who could resist such a move?" Boris asked me.

Boris' parents smiled whenever they heard the words "out in the country." Boris' girlfriend Irina hated country people. She hated everyone who wiped their ass with a corn cob and called "prrrrr" after their sheep. The only exception was her own father, whom she considered the smartest man in the world. Boris' parents didn't like Irina. Once when Boris and Irina were "breaking the Seventh Commandment" in the room, Aunty Maca kept clearing her throat and rapping on the door with a mop as she found it necessary to clean the floor right then and there... Boris opened the door. He got in her face:

"Fuck you and the broom you rode in on!"

Even though their noses almost touched, Boris' mother *didn't hear him*. She didn't hear him because what he said was not on the list of things possible in the universe. Maca gazed at Boris with an unchanged expression, as if he hadn't said anything.

When Irina ditched him, Boris went on a bender. He walked along the street with his head down. Not looking where he was walking, he bumped into a man in Terazije Square. Without raising his head, he moved him out of the way with an uppercut.

"I was sinking and sinking," he told me later. "I was waiting to hit bottom, so I could start reigniting my ambitions again."

Much later, when he learned that he and I had switched places and I was now going out with Irina, Boris didn't say a thing. Once we were drinking together, and I put my hand on his shoulder. He growled:

"Don't touch me."

"Why?" I asked.

Boris pointed both index fingers at himself:

"Because I'm crazy."

I pulled my hand back. It's difficult to quarrel with someone who can snap your arms and legs without breaking a sweat.

Boris graduated from a school of traffic engineering and started a business with Double Hulk. The business did well. Still, Boris quoted Confucius:

"All I see around me is Nothing that pretends to be Something, Emptiness that pretends to be Fullness, Dearth that pretends to be Plenty."

Boris started to gamble. To his father, who saved money by turning lights off around their apartment, he heatedly said:

"You entire monthly pension is less than one of my poker chips."

Irina remembered Boris fondly.

"When he wants to be, he's the funniest man in the world," she would say.

"Yes, he's funny," Bane admitted. "But he's a mean drunk."

"Boris never hesitates to quarrel with other people," I added. "This is how he thinks: We're going to fight sooner or later anyway. That's why it's better to do it sooner than later."

"That's because he's a mobster," Bane said.

"Well, he's always been like that," I noticed. "He was like that at school."

Bane shrugged:

"That means he was born a mobster."

CHAPTER 5

The unattainable Irina Bojović

When we were in high school, I couldn't find anything to talk about with Irina. Almond-eyed Irina would stand with a group of her girlfriends, and I would come by and say, "It's a nice day." Irina and her girlfriends would give me a look as if I had said something crude. Then Boris would come by and say, "It's a nice day," and they would simply melt.

"A nice day. Real nice!" they gushed. "Beautiful! Simply wonderful!"

I don't know what the problem was. Maybe I didn't twitch my eyebrows the right way. Screw it! To Irina and her girlfriends I was invisible. Just like the Russian poet Velimir Khlebnikov, I too

... in horror realized
That no one could see me
That eyes had to be sown
That an eye-sower must come

....

Back then, I was trying to become something but, as we all know, in this world one can only *be*, while *becoming* is frowned-upon. The whole world was an itch I wanted to scratch. I believed the Inquisition had created family as an instrument of torture. I was looking for a way to escape from the confines of high school, from the oppressive Sunday odor of stuffed sour cabbage rolls that permeated the apartment, from the TV's raucous sound of the Sunday soccer game. I went out for walks down Belgrade streets at two in the morning in hope I would meet "someone." I entered creaking elevators and pushed the top floor buttons hoping to reach the Moon. I hated to find that, all over Belgrade, elevators with wood paneling, crystal mirrors, and a bench upholstered with velvet were replaced by the *David Pajić* plywood atrocities.

Life wasn't bad in socialist Yugoslavia, but we were living a lie. On weekends, secretaries would fly to Rome and shop for clothes. In summer, construction workers would pull up their undershirts, slap their bellies, and growl: "You can't beat socialism." On TV, numbskulls babbled about what's "constructive" and what's "destructive." When I was young, everything interesting was considered suspicious. The mien of Yugoslav politicians revealed that boredom was a tool of social control. In spite of myself, I still remember some of their names. The most zealous brow-crinkler on TV was the Bosnian Branko Mikulić. He frowned at everyone's smile in this world. The Serbian Draža Marković sported a thin moustache of a provincial waiter, and we all expected him to rub his hands with delight and announce from the screen: "The tripe soup is especially good today." The Macedonian Krste Crvenkovski looked like a bat. The Slovene Stane Dolanc showed an uncanny resemblance to a hippopotamus.

I was perplexed by the appearance of the people who tailored our destiny. But my own photographs perplexed me as well because I didn't look real in them. The granite buildings that lined the canyon-like streets didn't look real either. I expected the celluloid tape of the Belgrade-and-me movie to snap on the reel and the buildings to dissolve into granular flashes and a rustle beyond reality. I craved to grab the tops of the buildings, pull myself up from the canyon of the street, and kiss the sky. I was suffocating.

And Irina?

To me, Irina was at once boring, unfathomable, and unattainable, and she looked like a being from Venus. I remember that she always introduced herself in two steps. First, she would say, "I'm Irina." Then she would thrust her chest out as if to say, "And these are my breasts." Whenever she did that, my legs would turn to jelly. What else can I say about her? "The well set nose" was considered a sign of great beauty in French ballads from the thirtheenth century. Irina's nose was well set.

That girl lived in the world of anti-matter. She dated *perfect* idiots. Because I read Rimbaud's *Illuminations*, her "perfect idiots" looked like older guys with cars. It was different when she hooked up with my friend Boris. Through Boris, Irina became a part of our family. But even before that, Bane grinned at me and panted into my ear:

"You're in love with her."

I don't know. It's possible that even in high school I had thought of her the way I did many years later. Even then, love may have raised her diamond whip above me – the flashiest and hardest of all whips. At times, I believed that a masochist would call Irina as sweet as pain. Had she been a hurricane, she could've sunk a thousand ships.

But Irina wasn't mine. Nothing in the world was mine. At that time, no one was from my planet. On the Post Office Building, I once saw graffiti with a line from a Belgrade *Dreams Manufac*ture song: "All the world is locked, and the keys are invisible." So true! – I exclaimed. Walls were all around me. All the doors were locked with invisible keys. High school classes were so boring I was ready to sell my soul to the devil just to change something. But – I often asked Bane – where can one find the devil in Belgrade on a Sunday afternoon?

CHAPTER 6

Bane Janović and the dream of the city

In the year of Our Lord 1921, on a horse-drawn street-car in Belgrade, Bane's great-grandfather Andrej Janović ordered a peasant to give him his seat.

"Fuck you," the peasant grumbled.

Bane's great-grandfather used his whip to reason with him. A second later, the Serbian peasant and the Russian aristocrat were rolling over the street-car floor enthusiastically trying to tear each other's throat out.

"This was an early sign that my family wouldn't do well in Belgrade," Bane sighed.

And they didn't.

Bane's ancestors were among those Serbs who, at the invitation of Catherine the Great, moved to the Ukraine in the eighteenth century. After the October Revolution, the family returned to the country they had left two centuries before. In Belgrade, Bane's great-grandfather Andrej drank his money away listening to the sad songs of Olga Jančevecka. Bane's father Ivan Janović didn't speak a word of Russian. The title of his doctoral dissertation was *The Motif of Barbecuing in Serbian Literature*. Ivan Janović was an abusive guy. He smacked the TV when it wasn't working right. He smacked his suitcase when it wouldn't fit into the trunk of his car. He smacked Bane too.

If you asked me how long I've known Bane, I would say: Forever! In kindergarten, I would tell him to eat an ant and he would eat it. In grade school, we had fun pulling girls' hair. Even though he moved to New Belgrade, we both attended Eighth High School.

We both shaved our heads in high school. After school, we were sitting at the *Our Suffering Café* in Čubura. I would ask him:

"If it was up to you to spare Alabama or Oklahoma from complete annihilation, which one would you choose?"

"I would spare Alabama. I don't give a shit about Oklahoma," Bane responded.

"Maybe Oklahoma is full of sensitive people and poets? Maybe the Alabamians are full of themselves?"

That's the kind of discussions we had.

Another time, Bane asked me:

"If a bull fought a rooster of comparable size, who would win?"

"Wait, the rooster would be the same size?"

"Yeah," Bane nodded his egg-shaped head.

"The rooster would win. It would peck the bull's eyes out."

We had these kinds of discussions.

When Bane became famous, we were all proud of him. His first album, *How Many of Them Do We Have and What*, was a family project. Bane and the saxophone player Marija wrote the music. Zora Stefanović designed the cover (which displayed the photo I took of Irina as Ophelia with water lilies in her hair). Boris acted as a manager and provided security at concerts.

Whenever Boris and Bane got together, they spoke in deep voices. Boris accused Bane of being "flippant." Bane only laughed in response. He not only showed his teeth but his gums too.

"Like a chimp," Boris said.

And yet, women would fall for Bane's melancholy eyes.

"Women will be the death of you," Zora warned him.

I envied Bane because of the girls who loved him. Even more so I envied him because, unlike me, he dared to be who he was. It seemed to me he had usurped the path in life that was meant for me. Due to his aristocratic frustrations, Bane envied me because my father, whom I barely knew, was a famous painter in Paris. He envied me because of our large apartment next to the Cathedral Church. He envied me because of my grandfather, an unbearable egotist who knew André Breton and belonged to the Belgrade Surrealist Movement.

Like many of our parents, Bane's father and stepmother thought they could be normal people and idiots at the same time, so in the long run they would somehow turn out to be normal. Whenever they had someone over for dinner, Bane's father tried to eat more than his guest. He called rock musicians "screaming faggots on drugs," and Bane liked it so much he almost considered it as a name for his band. Whenever Bane's stepmother saw a long-haired guitar player on TV, she didactically pontificated:

"Look at that idiot!"

Bane's father left his first wife and eloped with one of his students.

"She took a fancy to me," he explained. "She was young. What could I do?"

In the early days of his new relationship, Ivan Janović suffered a heart attack. As a convalescent, he went back to his first wife, so she could take care of him. When he recovered, he returned to his student. The ex-student became Bane's stepmother. When Bane's parents divorced, they traded their large apartment on Palmotićeva Street for two smaller ones. With his father, Bane moved to New Belgrade to the so-called *pavilions*—the yellow buildings full of cockroaches. After the divorce, Bane's mother went to America to stay with her uncle Nick Manović.

The situation in Yugoslavia was deteriorating, and Bane often considered moving to his mother's place in America.

His story changed in accordance to what he wanted to do on a particular day. When he felt like leaving, Belgrade would turn into a repugnant barbaric city where people walked around with bones in their noses. When he felt like staying, America would become a repugnant country without history where every third person was obese and politicians grinned like whales. He said:

"I don't want to go there, they don't sing the same songs."

"Unlike us, you at least have a choice," Zora encouraged him.

"Be careful, those who stay won't like those who leave," Irina cautioned him.

I shrugged my shoulders and told Boris:

"I can't figure Bane out."

"Of course you can't since he can't figure himself out," Boris scornfully smacked his lips.

Bane didn't leave, and we continued to drink beer in front of the ugly ziggurats of Block 63. I assume there was something beautiful about our hanging out there. We were drinking our beer and, motionless, rushed through the universe at the speed of nineteen miles per second, like everything else on this planet.

"Look at this," I encompassed the urban nothingness with a sweep of my hand. "These buildings rose up from the subconscious."

"You know what," Bane responded with a small cough. "If the design of the buildings of Block 63 in New Belgrade was inspired by Le Corbusier's theories, his remains should be exhumed and his bones shot out of a cannon."

I liked Bane because he didn't mind saying what everyone was thinking but wouldn't dare say. He looked out at the distance with those Cossack-like eyes of his and muttered:

"How strange life is…"

Gazing into the distance with a melancholy air, once he added:

"Last night I dreamed I founded a city. The city was whiter than a cuttlebone. It was whiter than chalk. It's strange but I didn't enter it; I turned my back to it and returned to the howling wilderness."

Engulfed within a halo of horror, I nearly choked. How could I tell him I had had the same dream at least ten times?

"So everyone dreams the same dream!" it dawned on me.

"This city too is strange," Bane continued. "I often wonder where in the world I live. I'd like to interview the city I live in."

Even though I'm a historian and Bane is a musician, I admit the idea was his.

Bane prompted me to do an interview with Belgrade.

CHAPTER 7

An interview with Belgrade

Question: How old are you?

Answer: At the time the Bajloni Brewery was being built, workers found a thirty thousand year old human skull and ten mammoth teeth. The owner of the ten mammoth teeth can be considered the oldest citizen of Belgrade.

Question: What makes you wonder?

Answer: I wonder about the Christian martyr Donatus (whom the Emperor Diocletian had strangled), who, on every seventh of January, arises from the Danube and wanders through my streets until dawn.

Question: City, whom do you belong to?

Answer: Since the beginning of time, nations have swirled around me like leaves in a whirlwind. Massacring each other, they have both razed and raised me. First, within my walls, Celtic Scordisaks sacrificed captured Romans to the gods. Then the Fourth Roman Legion rode out through my gates for four centuries. Flavius' Fourth Legion campaigned against Sarmatians and Dacians, Ostrogoths and Gepids. For a short period of time, Huns drove the Romans out of my gates. Mongolian Avars drove out Scandinavian Herulis from my vicinity. Led by the Avars, Slavs came like blind kittens. The glow of my walls opened their eyes, and they reconverted the fields around me again.

Armed with Greek fire, Byzantines fought Pechenegs and Hungarians over me. My new lovers became Bulgarians and Serbs who also razed and raised me. Tsintsars, Tartars, and Armenians came with the victorious Turks. After their expulsion from Spain and Hungary, Sephardic Jews clutched at my gates with a drowning hand. The great-grandchildren of the same Turks who captured me were already steeped in years when the Austrians first drove them out at the beginning of the never-ending Baroque wars. For centuries I, Belgrade, was a bone, and the Austrian and the Ottoman empires were dogs grappling over me and biting each other's jaws. When I became the Serbian principle city, many people moved in. Even more people moved in when I became the South Slavic capital. After the October Revolution exodus, one in four of my citizens were Russian.

Within me are Jewish, Ragusian, Armenian, Moslem, and Roman Catholic cemeteries. Their dead lie within my foundations. Their united prayers still protect me, even though they often failed to protect me when they were alive. Each nation and each individual were splinters in a maelstrom. All of them ate and prayed differently. From the Kalemegdan hill, all of them equally enjoyed the view of the birds above the waters. All equally loved the ridge above the rivers, rightfully called Meditation Hill. All those nations and individuals are your ancestors.

Question: What did those nations talk about?

Answer: They talked of love. They killed each other and constantly talked of love. "Love is an unrealized dream," the Herulis whispered. "In this world, love is impossible," growled the Avars. "Even here there's no love," the Serbs were stunned when my gates opened before them. "Love will be found in the Garden of Allah," the Turks said.

Question: Do you remember any saints and military leaders?

Answer: I remember that in me Diocletian passed the law regulating the appearance of witnesses in court. Jovian, who was born in me, reinstated Christianity to the Roman Empire, after Julian the Apostate banned it. Justinian rebuilt the Belgrade fortress and reinstated the bishoprics.

I, Belgrade, hosted the Slavic apostles Cyril and Methodius and also Angelar. St. Climent called me "the most glorious city on the Danube." For a while, I was the center of the heretical teaching named after the Presbyter Arius from Alexandria. On their way to the Crusades, Godfrey of Boulogne and – even more so – Walter of Pounce robbed me blind and burned me down. In me, Friedrich Barbarossa condemned those who perpetrated crimes in Hungary. John Hunyadi repelled the wounded conqueror of Constantinople, Mehmed II, from my walls. Within my walls, among the hosts of captured slaves, Suleiman the Magnificent was congratulated for conquering Hungary. Within my walls, the body of Suleiman the Magnificent lay in state after he had died. The relics of St. Sava were set on fire in me on April 27, 1594. The wind blew the ashes into the eyes of those present and many of the blind began to see. In me, Baron Trenk and Baron Münchausen played pharaoh at the *Wild Man Inn*.

Question: Do you remember your poets?

Answer: The Serbian Despot Stefan Lazarević, a Belgradian, composed his "Word on Love" in me. On the day of the despot-poet's death, the Bulgarian poet Constantine the Philosopher sang his "Cry, the white city, your blackest moment..." In me, the Jewish writer Yehuda Lerma lamented after the moments lost in the flow of time like "a tear in the rain." In me, Simha Cohen wrote down that "erudition isn't experience, and it doesn't free us from the need for experience." In me, Nurullah Muniri Belgradi wrote his treatise on Sadi. Drifting on a spring day as on a boat in the middle of a lake, he recorded: "The birds read, and the fishpond was their book. The winds wrote, and the clouds were their full stops..." The Serbian Patriarch Arsenius IV sent me the ominous line of warning: "The boar will devour your young..." In me wrote the bespectacled angel Dositej Obradović. In me, tossle-haired

Vladislav Petković Dis, with his nose pinched with a *pince nez*, droned his Symbolist verses:

> *It was last night that the dead came to me*
> *The old centuries and the graveyards new*
> *I was the victim they wanted to see*
> *An ephemeral, ever- fading hue.*

Question: Do you have any nick names?

Answer: The Romans called me Singidunum after the Celtic tribe the Sings. Apollonius of Rhodes named the Kalemegdan rock "Kanalak." Due to my Orthodox faith, the Austrians called me "Greek Belgrade." The Turks were the most creative with nick names. They called me "The Sultan's Wench," "The Rocky Foundation," "The House of Jihad," "The Heavenly Settlement," and "The Gates of War." As we all know, they called Kalemegdan "Meditation Hill." The most beautiful combination of all those nick names and my true name is:

> *Meditation Hill above the Gates of War.*

CHAPTER 8

The pillar of the world

I still can't tell you what to call me. I have a problem with documenting myself. Whenever a policeman asks to see my ID, I feel something twist in my guts.

I'm a historian. It's a dirty job, but someone's got to do it. I'm an honest historian (if that means anything). My heart is set not only on the wellbeing of my nation but on the wellbeing of all Balkan nations. Unasked, I'll tell you something about the Balkan nations—they don't have a clue about one another. Those nations are like overlapping drawings that, from a distance, look like a single drawing. That single drawing is beyond many of my fellow Balkan historians. Perhaps it's also beyond me, but I'm slowly ascending towards the vantage point from which I would be able to see it in its entirety. That's what's called academic research.

Unasked, I'll tell you something:

Had my mother and father asked me if they should marry, I would've told them: Don't! Had the people who created Yugoslavia, the country where I was born, asked me if they should create it, I would've told them: Don't! Children are born to bad marriages! To them, those bad marriages turn into the pillars of the world. Everywhere in the world parents lie to children, and the kids' ability to see through the lies is at the root of their painful process of growing up. I asked my friend Zora Stefanović why they lie to children everywhere in the world.

"First, because their parents often don't know any better," the insightful Zora responded. "Second, because families, states, and ideologies are based on half-truths at best, and a germ of a lie grows better in a truth than a germ of a truth grows in a delusion."

I think that Zora is right. Be aware of the curious fact that a union between two fools may create that which is called the family, and a union of a larger number of fools may create that which is called the state. Such trite, poorly constructed structures like the state and the family may be the Pillar of the World to someone—me, for example, who mulls over all of this with an air of superiority.

What is the Pillar of the World?

Mircea Iliade writes—for the life of me I don't know in which book—about the Pillar of the World. That's a totem—for the life of me I don't know of what tribe—that links the sky and the earth. Mircea Eliade says that, when the totem is destroyed, the members of the tribe lie down around their ruined Pillar of the World and die. Such things happen when the fragile construction that supports someone's sky is demolished. Some of my relatives and friends died when the house of cards we lived in—Yugoslavia—collapsed. Just like that. They lay down and died.

At the end, I'll remind you that I can't tell you who I am. What I'm writing about is the fruit of my speculation which can't be called academic. This is a story about one love of mine, three friendships, one horrible war or a series of wars, the desolution of the idea of homeland, the continuing weakening and loss of support, the explosive fragmentation of the world, the forgotten Byzantine mosaic technique, the mirror for the reflection of the soul and my endeavors to use other people and my city as a mirror. This is also a story about an eternal process of founding the city, about cannibals and beauties, people who pat tigers—and many other minor characters. Of course, minor characters never see themselves that way. Just like the author of this true story, they refer to themselves as:

"I."

This is sort of a public diary which I'm writing with the intention of maybe publishing it someday. I've already admitted that I'd like to unite different, often disparate details of my life in this diary. Each of my fingers is threaded to one of those details. Sometimes I feel like a puppeteer controlling the details. Sometimes I'm a puppet twitching on the strings. Since I don't want to reveal my name, I'll have to use a different one in these pages.

When I defended my doctoral dissertation, my friend Boris jokingly called me Doctor Jekyll. I believe that's a good, solid quip. I don't mind being called that. Let the name stay. Ha, ha. I'm really happy with the choice.

Doctor Jekyll.

***

But what's this, in God's name?

I wrote down those lines, rather pleased with myself. Then I put the notebook aside, dozed off, and fantasized about Irina's panties. I came to, took up the notebook, and started to read again. There was a mirror hanging on the wall next to me. Its all-seeing eye reflected a page from my diary. I looked and saw that the letters in the mirror weren't reversed—there was something quite different from what I wrote.

This is what was written:

CHAPTER 8
IN THE MIRROR

Which heralds the rant about the Millennium

This idiot has finally fallen asleep. Phew! "My heart is set on the wellbeing…" What a fool! Sharing a body with such a fool is so exasperating! No doubt you wonder who I am. If he's the Overt Gentleman, I'm obviously the Covert Gentleman! My name is Mr. Hyde. Let me tell you what *my* heart is set on. My heart is set on the Millennium!

The beginning of the Millennium is the moment when the blazing star falls down and a third of the waters becomes blood. The earth moves and the volcanos erupt. Animals stampede. Fields turn black with locusts. Baboons howl for days. People see shape-shifting dogs. Each day begins to resemble a black carnival. People are thrilled, so thrilled! Oh! The Millennium is thrilling and so are the comets that shoot across the sky day and night. Women's skirts grow ever shorter. Men stop wearing pants and dogs start wearing them. The sun doesn't set for days. Light becomes even more intense from the ceaseless eruptions. Instead of daily news, newspapers print only omens and small newspaper boys go around shouting:

"Omens! Omens!"

People become excitable and they easily sweat. Every now and then one reads about some slaughtered priest. It should be pointed out that people also start speaking in tongues they don't know. That's what I'm trying to do too – on these pages at the time of the Millennium. I'm trying, oh my brothers, to speak in a tongue I don't know. My own tongue!

CHAPTER 9

A less-strange-than-true episode concerning me and Irina

When I ran into the almond-eyed Irina on the Zemun promenade, I heard a soft "click" and realized that, between us, something changed. Those dark eyes, that used to reveal only indifference, now showed an interest. Maybe I became interesting as the future owner of a large apartment in the best part of the city. Maybe she had seen me a couple of times on TV as I was arguing that the Balkan nations only pretended to believe in different gods while they all worshipped the same god – Passion. Maybe my spade-shaped goatee suited me well. I wouldn't be the grandson of the Belgrade Surrealist painter Teofil Đorđević without believing in the simplest of all explanations – *the miracle*. On that day, the miracle yanked the ground beneath our feet like a carpet. For the first time Irina told me something about herself.

"Up until the end of high school, I was swimming out on the wide sea with no land in sight. Then... very slowly... the coastline came into view."

That afternoon I realized how little we know about the people we think we know well! It turned out that, in high school, Irina had a problem with heroin.

"I had no clue," I was stunned.

"I thought everyone knew," Irina sighed.

Irina had a picture taken with a group of friends on the day they started rehab. She was convinced they would all be able to get off heroin. Except for Irina, all the young people in the photograph are now dead. The last time she saw Biljana and Deki, they were two emaciated ghosts very gently supporting each other on a bus. Later she came across their obituaries in *Politika*.

"I don't like that people are mortal," Irina shuddered. "It's uncomfortable thinking about it alone in the night."

Irina confessed she wasn't particularly ambitious regarding the afterlife – she didn't expect to end up in Heaven. She believed Limbo was good enough for her.

When her father Čedomir Bojović learned that his daughter was on drugs, he sent her to the renowned doctor Popov in Moscow. Doctor Popov made Irina hate her life, but he freed her from heroin addiction. For a long time upon her return to Belgrade, whenever she walked by the places where she used to shoot up, Irina had the feeling we have when we pass an ex-lover's apartment.

"Shivering is the right word to describe the state I was in for a year," she admitted.

"How come Boris never mentioned that to me?"

Irina shrugged.

Engrossed in conversation, we climbed to Upper Town and took a walk through the Zemun cemetery. I showed her the statue of a girl with a narrow waist and enormous breasts. I happened to know that Zemun middle-schoolers would come to the cemetery and masturbate to the curves of that bronze beauty.

"That proves that female beauty lives beyond the grave," Irina smiled.

We had coffee at the Sibinjanin Janko Tower. I insisted that Zemun looks the best from a boat on the river as it gleams in the suddenly expanded space. I felt my soul expanding as the ice melted between us.

"You know I had a crush on you in high school," I confessed.

"Why didn't you ever tell me?"

Now it was my turn to shrug.

We went down the cobble-stone street to the restaurant *Šaran*. At *Šaran* we had a shot of apricot brandy and then ordered some fish stew. A guy with baggy eyes entered the restaurant's courtyard hawking cheap jewelry and wind-up mice that ran across the table cloth. I bought Irina a wind-up mouse, and we went for a stroll along the Zemun promenade. As we walked, a warm amniotic bubble formed around us. Something made us rub shoulders and elbows as we walked. The wind was blowing off the gilded patches on the Danube. The boats were in the sun.

Irina looked at the big light in the sky, blinked and smiled. She called that "kissing the Divine Eye."

"On a day like this, the sun moves into you," she said. "You just glide by like the sun."

"Maybe this is one of the most beautiful moments in my life," I thought.

Irina said how, officially, she despised women's magazines that contained pictures of beauties who were uncertain whether to throw seductive glances or flash brilliant smiles. And yet, she admitted that she regularly stole such magazines from her mother and with utmost interest read about "ten things you should never do naked" or "how attraction turns into love" or "five new color designs for the summer" or "how to make a refreshing cucumber salad." After she had read every single word, she returned the magazine to her mother's room like a thief, and resumed her attitude of intellectual superiority.

"There's a sense of genuine vitality about those magazines," I concurred.

I told her that my boss at the Institute of Balkan History was a stickler who looked like a tapir. I talked about doubts I had regarding my professional field, history. My boss loved statistics. I claimed that opinions can't be replaced by numbers. What could we conclude about the nature of Christianity, I wondered, if we learned about the percentage of Jewish men, ages twenty five to thirty five, who considered themselves living gods?

According to one of the gnostic theories, God created the world with his laughter. I thought I heard an echo of that divine laughter in the laughter with which Irina responded to my words.

Irina confessed she had never told a man she loved him. After all the years we spent together, I found out she had never uttered those words to me either.

We walked all the way to the confluence of the Sava and the Danube and went to the Museum of Contemporary Art. As we looked at the paintings, Irina told me that her little sister Sanja exuded confidence. Whenever someone told her she was beautiful, Sanja glanced down and acknowledged:

"Yes, I'm beautiful."

When they told her she was smart, she agreed:

"Yes, I'm very smart."

"Were you like that when you were little?" I wanted to know.

Irina pondered:

"To tell you the truth, I think I was. Later I changed."

The day was still brilliant when we came out of the Museum of Contemporary Art. I looked westward and saw the contours of the city imprinted on a hot copper plate. The day with Irina was beautiful, and the sunset was even more so. The sky shimmered. The ground was radiant. As I walked her to the bus stop, my heart boomed like the bell of the Cathedral Church. People turned and looked at me. I couldn't take my eyes off of Irina. The sunny mist still lingered in the corners of her eyes and lips. If Apollonius of Rhodes was asked to describe the state I was in, he would write that Cupid, sent by Aphrodite, pierced my heart with his arrow. He set it ablaze while my soul melted in sweet pain.

I promised myself I would never forget that day in April 1988. Certainly this wasn't an everyday experience. I wondered if our feelings were mutual. Someone said that everything is always mutual. From experience, I knew it wasn't, but I liked the idea of it.

"Only once in my life I felt this way," Irina stated. "When I took ecstasy."

I coughed.

"There could be a more flattering name for that drug."

I didn't know what I was trying to say, but we both laughed. We waited for something. As we waited, she missed two buses. For a long time I was hesitant to touch her as if she was protected by an alarm system. But eventually I felt the softness of Irina's lips and was granted the right to acquaint my hands with her body. Everything started to dance at that moment. I was a lover. I was someone from *A Thousand and One Nights*.

Later, I frequently visited Irina and drank whisky with her father Čedomir Bojović. Čedomir once asked me how we started dating. I told him we accidentally ran into each other on a long and beautiful day. I walked her home and we missed two buses as I gathered the courage to kiss her. It took me more courage to kiss Irina than it took Double Hulk to fight some Bulbuder scum.

"And what kind of courage did it take Double Hulk to fight the Bulbuder scum?" Irina's father Čedomir was interested.

I raised my finger vigorously and exclaimed:

"Great courage!"

CHAPTER 10

Intriguing stories featuring Double Hulk

"When Double Hulk headed to a show-down with the Bulbuder scum, times were different," I explained to Irina's father Čedomir Bojović. "Instead of guns, toughs had knives. When Double Hulk headed to a show-down with the Bulbuder scum, his brother was in prison. His future best man, my good friend Boris, was in the military."

Double Hulk was alone.

Preparing for the show-down, Double Hulk donned a black duster. Under it, he hid his and his brother's spear-guns. He cut the harpoon lines. At the site of the show-down – just like in *High Noon* – Double Hulk strode towards two toothless assholes, the Vukotić brothers, and their friend Abaga. Abaga was a man with a broken nose and a cauliflower ear; his chin directly rested on his chest because God forgot to give him a neck.

"What d'you want, you piece of shit?" Abaga welcomed Double Hulk. "Now we're gonna poke your eyes out."

Abaga and the younger Vukotić flashed their knives. The older Vukotić was slapping his palm with a metal bar. Double Hulk waited for the Vukotićes and Abaga to come closer. Then he pulled out one spear-gun. Mercifully aiming at the legs, he hit the older Vukotić in the knee and crippled him for life. With a grim smile, Double Hulk pulled out the other spear-gun. He clutched it with both hands and aimed at Abaga's chest. The little Vukotić threw away his knife and ran. The older Vukotić never forgot how he helplessly called after his younger brother:

"Don't leave me, Mijo."

Step by step, Abaga backed up. He kept saying: "Don't do it, Nebojša, I beg you." It seemed to Double Hulk that the degenerate Abaga spoke to him with the voice of his dead mother Desanka: "Don't do it, Nebojša, I beg you." He put down the gun and said:

"Go home."

After he let Abaga go, Double Hulk approached the wounded Vukotić and kicked him in the teeth. This episode earned him his first jail term.

"If I turned a deaf ear to my dead mother and killed Abaga, I would've certainly spent more time in the slammer," he said later.

"But then we wouldn't have to deal with the Vukotićes and Abaga," Boris said with a frown.

Before I met Boris' friend, I didn't know that the human chin can look like a block of marble. When Double Hulk came back from prison, I asked him innocently:

"Are there good people in prison?"

He focused his dark eyes on me:

"Yeah. But not many."

Double Hulk loved to tell stories about prison. On the wall of his cell, someone wrote: "Woe to him who believes." Double Hulk played soccer with some geezer from Paraćin, who was in for twenty years. Caught up in the game, the old man embraced him and said: "I love you like my own son." The problem was that he killed his own son in a drunken rage. Double Hulk remembered a tough from Vinkovci who started to read the Bible in the big house. That's where he realized it was a book of great power. He realized that God was tougher than any tough guy from Vinkovci or Belgrade. That's why he turned to the Bible. In addition to his stories from prison, Double Hulk also liked to give me advice about women:

"A woman likes to get slapped once in a while," he lectured me. "A woman must never think she's figured you out. When she thinks you'll kiss her, slap her, and when she thinks you'll slap her – kiss her. This is how you make the chick think: See, I can't pin him down."

That profound masculine philosophy reminded me of the feminine philosophy that Irina expostulated to me:

"Whenever a man wants to get close to me, I become more distant. Constantly out of his reach."

Both before and after prison, Double Hulk had issues with the police because of bar fights. Double Hulk tried to make me believe he was always the victim. His take on these incidents was always the same. He would peacefully sit in a bar and sip his drink. A guy would come in and start to rudely insult him. Double Hulk would try to make the bully see that his behavior was inappropriate:

"Buddy, don't talk like that, it's not nice."

The guy would continue to rudely and heedlessly insult him.

Double Hulk would warn the thug again:

"Don't do this, buddy. We'll have to mix it up."

The guy would continue with his obnoxious harrasment.

Not being able to put up with this revolting treatment, Double Hulk would jump up, grab the jerk by the nose and the seat of his pants and throw him out through the bar window. Because he was so aggitated, he would also rough up the bartender and two other young men sitting at the table next to him.

"I did everything within my power to prevent that from happening," he innocently spread his arms when the bar filled up with cops.

At one point, Irina complained to Boris that three kids from her apartment building were acting like jerks. Not only did they ogled her – they also played very loud music till dawn. One day, their loudspeakers made our ears bleed while we were all sitting in Irina's room. Boris got annoyed and stood up.

"Boris, please don't go," Zora wailed.

"It won't be me."

Boris dialed a number:

"Double Hulk? It's Boris. I'm at Irina's. Please come as soon as you can!"

A half hour later, with an explosion of hellish music, the three brothers opened the door. The sun eclipsed. Double Hulk was standing in the doorway. His hairy head and beard looked like those of a Babylonian winged bull. Double Hulk scratched his nose and said with that fake good natured voice of his:

"Listen, guys. My uncle lives next door. He's an elderly gentleman. He can't sleep because of your music. My uncle's upset. How would you feel if you couldn't sleep? That would be awful. No one wants that…"

Stammering, the guys apologized… After that, Irina's apartment building was filled with a silence deeper than that of the Kalahari Desert. After he became proficient in judo, Double Hulk stopped brawling. He opened a flower shop across the street from Central Cemetery and employed an army of Gipsy kids to steal flowers from graves for him. He resold the flowers. Three different funerals were graced with the same bouquet. Double Hulk could never have enough money, so he started smuggling leather jackets from Istanbul and electronic appliances from Munich. At first, Boris worked with him, but he soon started to complain how he was wasting his time and it was embarrassing.

Double Hulk had a brother named Dada, whom Zora and I were scared of because he had eyes as dead as coffee beans. The anus of a horse in a Paolo Uccello painting was much more expressive than the eyes of that man. Dada was wanted in several European countries. From time to time, he put on a Kevlar vest, got on a plane, and flew away to kill one of the "enemies of Yugoslavia" in Munich or Zurich. Then he returned to Belgrade and calmly resumed tending to his café-bar. Dada was one of the early examples of the overlap between the secret service and the mob. When the war started, Boris and Double Hulk, in collusion with Dada, began to bring in semi-truck trailers full of who-knows-what from Croatia and gasoline tankers from Romania. All the time during the period of the most severe shortages, when Yugoslavia was under sanctions, Double Hulk traded in gasoline. In fits of arrogance, he left his white Mercedes with its engine running in front of his café-bar. It would idle there for a couple of hours. At a time when gasoline was sold by bottles in Belgrade, when people didn't have enough to drive to the hospital, a pensioner approached Double Hulk's table and timidly pointed out:

"Sir, your engine is running."

Double Hulk winked and said with his fake good natured voice:

"You worry too much about life, old man. You'll have a heart attack. Let it run."

This is almost the entire story concerning Double Hulk. Much of what I have mentioned happened later on. To Irina's father Čedomir Bojović, I just told the first part. When I finished, Čedomir blinked in dissatisfaction and said:

"The courage Double Hulk needed to accept the duel with the Bulbuder scum and, don't mind me smiling, the courage you needed to kiss Irina – is no courage at all."

CHAPTER 11

On the liberation of Belgrade

Having said that neither Double Hulk nor I could crow about our courage, Irina's father victoriously took a sip of whiskey.

"What do you mean?" I asked.

"Compared to the courage we needed to liberate Belgrade, that's no courage at all."

"All right then, Mr. Čedomir, what kind of courage did you need to liberate Belgrade?"

Čedomir Bojović's gaze focused past his raised finger and he said:

"Great."

"Will you tell me something about it?"

"I will…"

"Will you do it now?"

"I will. In October 1944, my brigade came from Sanjak by way of Užice and Suvobor. We descended on the city from Dedinje. That was the first time we saw such a large city. Even Kruševac and Niš used to look like big cities to us. At that time, the city was turned into a fortress. You ask what kind of courage was needed to liberate Belgrade? First, in a city, you don't know where the shots are coming from. Your head is ringing and you are turning around like a weather vane because they can hit you from anywhere."

The Germans barricaded themselves in buildings and secured the entrances with trip wires. Many people were killed by anti-tank and anti-personnel mines. Russians advanced with their mine detectors and marked safe passages for their tanks. The forefather of all future Belgrade graffiti, an inscription in Russian, "ALL CLEAR, NO MINES," appeared on buildings.

All of Belgrade was a ruin. Buildings were either completely destroyed or badly damaged. Many looked like pyramids made of bricks. I believe that future parks and parking lots were built on the sites of obliterated structures. The Prince Mihailo Monument was riddled with bullets. The National Theater building was badly peppered with gunfire, especially around the windows.

Bunkers smoldered at crossroads. A horrible stench rose from the bunker next to the Officers' Club. Piles of bloated and grinning corpses were there. Everything was looted, razed, shut down. Only the Belgradians were happy as they took up arms. They would come to us running to let us know: The Germans are over there, that's where they're shooting from. Then, we would attack that building. You ask what kind of courage I needed to liberate Belgrade? When heavy machinegun fire starts to raise dust around you and your ears are filled with explosions, you can't control your own body. You are lying down, but you are trembling so much that you flop on the sidewalk like a fish. Fear is a natural state of mind and it's unnatural to restrain it. It's unnatural, but possible. Along with the Russians, we crawled towards the windows through which heavy machineguns barked. Together, we tried to drag the wounded away from cross fires. I witnessed two partisans and a Russian die as they tried to rescue one of our wounded.

Many Germans were buried by the Ministry of Railroads. The small park in front of that building is in fact a graveyard. I always think of that whenever I pass by it. This is just an offhand remark. The combat slowly tapered off. The liberators started to dance. With our arms spread out and interlocked, we and the Russians looked like a bunch of crucified Jesuses dragging one another in a ring dance. I joined a ring dance in front of a building at the end of

French Street. We were unaware that a steady eye watched us down a cannon barrel from a window on the third floor.

A German officer raised a light cannon from the backyard with a coal pulley, positioned it at the window, and covered it with curtains. The cannon fired and recoiled back into the room. Our dead and wounded were left to lie on the sidewalk. We ran for cover and opened fire. They responded with a heavy machinegun from above, so we flattened our noses to the ground. A fair-haired Russian took his time aiming his mortar. His shell jumped up and through the window on the third floor like a flea.

An explosion! – Čedomir Bojović spread his arms with a dramatic flair.

Silence! – with both hands, the narrator gently rubbed something invisible.

When we looked up, we saw smoke billowing through the window. The scattered dancers gathered together and pointed to the window on the third floor. Later, a few of us climbed up. We threw two dead bodies out of the window and into the yard. The mortar shell demolished one room, but the other two were fine. I told my comrades that it was better to spend the night in that apartment rather than in the four-layered bunks in the lobby of the Law School where we were stationed. The lobby wasn't heated. We were lucky that the weather was dry. By the way, we – the liberators of Belgrade – went for a meal of beans and corn bread at the mess which was stationed in the building of the Academy of Arts and Sciences. I remember that they put some captured German marmalade into our mess-kits, which we thought an extravagant luxury. And so we decided to spend a night in a liberated apartment of a liberated city.

"He's making it all up," I thought.

Čedomir Bojović drank his whiskey with gusto, cleared his throat, and continued:

I've already told you that we and the Russians were on quite good terms and that we rescued each other's wounded. That's true. And yet… That evening, something happened that could've cost me may rank and perhaps my life. Several of us lay down on the floor in the large room using a rug for a blanket. I watched my comrades as they slept. I watched them thinking – young guys, fatigued, primitive. What can you do, they were bumpkins, but they had good hearts. At that moments, I heard screams from the bathroom:

"Help! Don't!"

I rushed in there and saw the fair-haired Russian assaulting a girl by the name of Milojka. He had already ripped off her shirt made of parachute silk and started to yank off her pants. I was just a kid back then, you know. I was one of those communist ideologues, and I would ride on a white horse into liberated towns, but I was totally clueless as to what was going on. To us Yugoslav communists, Russians were bigger than life. That's how we were taught. Russians were selfless, devoted beings from a superior world. I grabbed the Russian, Kolya, whom I had known well from before, by the arm and said:

"Wait a minute, comrade. We make love too, but not like that…"

He drunkenly looked at me and growled in Russian:

"Get out, you motherfucker. I liberated you."

A bloody maelstrom of all my years as a guerilla fighter swirled in my head. I cried in pain:

"You liberated who?"

He reached for his handgun. I was faster. I put my American Colt to his head. Two thoughts ran through my head: "A revolver won't jam," and "I killed a Russian."

I somehow managed to disarm him and pushed him out of the apartment. I locked the door and barricaded it. That was how I spent the first night in the apartment that would later become my own. I specifically asked for that apartment, and the authorities then assigned it to me. My ex-wife Olga now lives there.

CHAPTER 12

The importer

I always tried to figure him out. I was a frequent guest at his house in Neimar. Over drinks, I learned a great deal about his life. Even more so through Olga's stories...

Čedomir Bojović was born in the village of Ribnica near Kraljevo. During World War II, the German occupation forces in Kraljevo would execute one hundred civilian hostages for every German soldier killed. The steel helmets gathered hostages in factories and pulled out stunned students from schools. Čedomir was also taken out with his high school classmates. As he was led to his execution with his mouth agape, it occurred to him:

"Fuck them. Let them kill me!"

The boy who would become Irina's father, bounced down a slope like a boulder, leaped over a hedge, and ran away through well known backyards. He was seventeen when his uncle helped him join the partisans. For the rest of his life, his right shoulder remained lower than his left from carrying a rifle. He was captured in a skirmish and taken to Belgrade. In prison, they beat the soles of his feet and scraped his shins. Čedomir didn't give anyone up.

"What matters is not in the soles and shins," he explained to me. "It's in the hearts and souls."

When they were transferring Čedomir Bojović from one Belgrade prison to another, a dozen flat hats armed with guns blocked the street. They pulled out the prisoners from the police truck and put them in their own truck. Clipping the corners, they whipped around the city till they reached the safety of a garage. Through partisan channels, Čedomir once more joined the guerillas. He became a political commissar when he was nineteen. There's a photograph from 1944 in which Čedomir is entering a liberated city riding on a white horse.

After the war, Čedomir Bojović was assigned to the position of the chief military intelligence officer in Kikinda. In his first week on the job, the famous war hero Mićan Brbanović Žvane died during surgery in Kikinda. People don't die from a routine appendectomy. The war hero was in excellent health. The surgeon had good credentials. There were two nuns assisting during the operation. The case was turned over to Čedomir Bojović. Irina's father had to really walk on egg shells there because the communist authorities were in the early stages of reestablishing relationships with the Roman Catholic Church. What now, he asked himself. Cigarette ends scorched his fingernails. He paced around his office in the yellow light of a bare bulb. At two in the morning, he shouted out in the hallway:

"Bring the nuns over to me!"

They brought in a nun with cheeks like peaches and dim blue eyes. Bobbing his head, Čedomir approached her. Then he started to knock her around the room with his fists.

"How did you kill him?"

The woman screamed:

"Stop, sir, I'll tell you everything!"

It turned out that the nuns poisoned the gauze that was used during the procedure. They were Croatian Nazi sympathizers. They were executed at dawn and Čedomir was transferred to Belgrade. In Belgrade he was able to have the apartment he liberated assigned to him. The first night he stayed there, he dreamed a strange dream:

He dreamed of bookstores and tea-shops where a man could comfortably grow old. He dreamed of a place that seduced him with details and made him fall in love with the whole. He dreamed of a city being continually established in the dreams of its citizens yet failing to be established. That was a city of eternal noon, without twilight and shadows. Angels strolled through the streets, and from windows women showered them with confetti from pillow-cases. The political commissar of not long ago, Čedomir Bojović woke up covered in sweat and swore:

"Never again will I have pork steak and Greek salad for dinner."

For Čedomir Bojović, the third of September 1948 was historically much more important than the Cominform Resolution and Tito's break with Stalin. On the third of September, Čedomir's absolute belief in Marxism-Leninism was challenged. This is how it happened: Čedomir took a certain actress out for dinner. After dinner, he kissed her in the entryway to a building. He slipped his hand underneath her skirt and felt her silk panties. The texture of silk beneath his fingers diminished the authority of Marx and Engels' teaching. The discovery of the previously unknown item of female wardrobe fundamentally shook up the foundations of Čedomir's worldview. That was his Copernican shift. He was never the same person again.

As a part time student, Čedomir Bojović graduated from the School of Law and started working in one of the first Yugoslav import-export firms which here I will call Manex Export. My friend Boris believed that Irina's father's entire export-import business was a façade. He winked and repeated:

"Once a cop – always a cop."

One must admit that Čedomir Bojović's conclusions regarding foreign trade were not uninteresting:

"All ignoramuses," he sighed. "Three people wouldn't make one competent individual. But don't think that those working for our foreign partners are demigods either. No way! The same jackasses as here! Only a few people do all the real work for everyone else as well. The only difference is that some of them dare to be clever. That's allowed over there…"

Abroad, Čedomir Bojović made a good impression because he wasn't dogmatic. He knew how to be charming when the job warranted it. He liked to go to Italy on business. He would do the job in five days but stay for fifteen. In Yugoslavia they asked him what it was he imported.

"I import common commodities," he responded with a smile. "But I'd rather import some charm. We need a lot of charm."

Čedomir's friends utilized the large apartment in Dorćol to entertain the fairer sex. So many had an opportunity to scrutinize the ceiling there! You would be shocked if I gave you the list of their names.

"I tell women that I love them," Čedomir would laugh in the company of his fellow philanderers. "That always relaxes the atmosphere."

One year Čedomir went to Dubrovnik "for his health" and came back with a young woman who lovingly called him "my blue eyes." Čedomir's young wife was soon able to dismiss the bunch of good-for-nothings who besieged the apartment in Dorćol. In her imagination, Olga knocked on the doors of the little sluts who orbited around Čedomir and asked them: Are you Lela, Sanja, Maja? They responded in the affirmative. Without saying another word, Olga pulled out a Luger and fired into their seductive faces and tantalizing stomachs. That's how it looked in her imagination. In reality, she was able to repel all females from her threshold and to turn Čedomir into a hamster who would hoard beautiful and useful things and bring them back from his trips abroad. Olga contributed by buying old lamps and antiquities at the Bajloni market.

In their first year, the bed collapsed under Čedomir and Olga. The young spouses brought in a carpenter and told him to support the frame with a fifth leg in the middle. Čedomir was happy with his marriage. His job at Manex Export caused him headaches. Ruling over the Manex Export human herd wasn't easy. Each one of them considered a meeting a failure if they didn't "discuss the issues" for half an hour. Čedomir's secretary was an evil coquette who slept with all the men from the neighboring offices. His subordinates were boring. In meetings, one boasted about eating roasted pork for breakfast while another one expressed regret about not eating it. The subordinates had a proclivity for writing anonymous memos. Čedomir's good buddy asked him to come over to the offices of the City Communist Party Committee and showed him a few such missives. They claimed that Chairman Bojović acted as if he personally invented Mercedes cars, Johnny Walker whiskey, and German goose liver pate. The anonymous memos asserted that he didn't differentiate between the Party ideals and personal benefits. (What ideal is higher than personal benefits? – an anonymous author asked wittily.) Ultimately, the anonymous letters claimed that Čedomir Bojović embezzled money from the Italian branch of the company which was registered in his name.

"Do you believe that?" Čedomir asked in a hoarse voice.

"If we did, we wouldn't have shown them to you," his good buddy from the Committee responded.

Čedomir went back to his office and called a special Party meeting.

"Comrades, we've noted certain trends," with those words he opened the meeting. "There have been certain elements among us who work against the interest of our firm. What do we call such elements, comrades?" he asked while his raised index finger gleamed like a radioactive rod. Twenty frightened male and female heads blankly stared at him, mouths agape. In triumph, Čedomir pierced the air with his index finger and roared like a lion: "We call them rumor-mongers!"

Whomever Čedomir Bojović addressed that day started to stammer. The meeting's outcome was the recall of the representative from Rome. One person got fired. A few independent division heads were demoted to menial posts. They tried to conspire against him.

"Let them conspire," Čedomir said with a small smile. "The only thing they can lose is their shackles."

Čedomir Bojović remained the head of Manex Export. He kept importing and importing. He imported inky, lead-colored clouds from New England. He imported crystal-clear dawns from Japan. He imported rains from South California. He imported bloody sunsets from Goa. Thanks to him, we had all those things in Belgrade.

Chairman Bojović occasionally went to Kalemegdan to play a game of chess with the beak-like noses of ex-partisans from Kordun, the disillusioned ones who talked about their brigades. Together, they would loudly denounced thieving politicians.

At the same time Čedomir Bojović first strengthened his position in Manex Export, he and Olga started to fight horribly.

"What held you back for so long?" Čedomir's friends wondered.

He shrugged his shoulder:

"Screwing."

When the sexual attraction between Olga and Čedomir diminished after ten years of marriage, everything became a problem. It was as if they saw each other for the first time. Olga claimed that Čedomir deliberately snored when he slept with her and didn't snore when he slept in another room. Just like Boris' father, Čedomir turned off lights to save electricity. It so happened he turned off the light when Olga was in the bathroom.

"Turn it on, you idiot!" she hollered.

"Sorry, I thought…" Čedomir mumbled behind the door.

Olga loved to go to the movies and cry while watching them. Čedomir told her:

"Calm down, those are just actors. They're paid well for doing that."

"You pig, you ruin everything I like," Olga was annoyed.

Olga and Čedomir had different Rh factors. That cost them their first baby. They tried again. Despite all the measures to save her pregnancy, the second child was also stillborn. Olga went out with their children's ghosts and came back with them. In her imagination, those two spirits were swallows who built a nest in the corner of their room. The marriage turned into a desert island for the marooned couple. The husband and wife didn't have anything to say to each other anymore.

When Olga fell in love with my father Andrija, Čedomir filed for a divorce and left her the apartment. Soon after, he married a girl who would become Irina's mother. Čedomir's mother-in-law's maiden name was Talvi and her house in Neimar was built with the money from the "one hundred box cars of trousers" transaction by the Talvi & Mandilović Company. On the terrace of that house, I had my share of the stories from Čedomir's life. This was sort of a holy neighborhood because Mullah Pasha burned St. Sava's relics nearby in 1594. According to the legend, the wind carried the ashes toward a group of beggars and ten blind people regained their sight…

In the holy neghborhood, in the house overgrown with ivy, Čedomir had his daughter Irina. Unfortunately, his daughter's birth didn't settle his spirit down. He spent more time in business meetings and on business trips than at home. On those trips, Čedomir Bojović had attacks of wolfish hunger. His humongous appetite fit a starving Ethiopian or someone from Sudan rather than a fat chairman of a foreign trade firm. When he was hungry, Čedomir Bojović started to hiss. His driver ducked his head between his shoulders and whispered:

"If he could only satisfy his hunger…"

Čedomir's driver abruptly pulled up in front of the first restaurant and obliginly opened the back door. Chairman Čedomir rushed out. In a silent movie, his exit would be followed by the subtitle "The Beast Has Been Released." In the restaurant, Čedomir ordered a never ending train of dishes. He guarded his plate with his elbows and, with his mouth full, mumbled the words of Branko Ćopić:

"I'm eating for my father and for my grandfather and for all of my hungry relatives…"

Just like the great writer, Čedomir didn't only eat. He also drank. He drank without any pangs of guilt up until he came across Tin Ujević's lines:

Those many years I wasn't alive
My entire being grew numb
And grasp on life got twisted awry
So I slept in the street like a bum…

After he had read the verses' warning, Čedomir went to complain to his psychiatrist friend. The psychiatrist heard him out with a smile. Then he became serious and said:

"I can't help you. You're an alcoholic."

"Well, offer me a drink then," Čedomir sighed.

The doctor poured them drinks and concluded:

"Our mistake is that we approach an alcoholic as if they were sick. We're trying to understand the circumstances of their life and all that. Instead, we should tell them: You're a jerk and an asshole.

So, jerk, stop ruining yourself and everyone around you. That's what they should be told. To your health…"

Focused on his glass, Čedomir hesitated. He mustered the strength to say:

"To health…"

And he downed it in one gulp.

CHAPTER 13

"Oh how I long to bathe my burning heart in the freezing spring of your heart"

My mother Milena specialized in children's diseases and worked at the Mother and Child Institute in Zemun. Irina's mother Dafina was a homemaker. And yet, Dafina looked down on my mother as if she was a pretentious petit bourgeois. Dafina never felt comfortable sitting under the needlepoints with the well-known motifs of "Town Covered with Snow" and "Horses at the Waterhole" in my mother's apartment. Čedomir liked Milena because she was from Kraljevo and because he sighed with satisfaction at her dinner table. Milena and Čedomir reminisced about the willows on the banks of the Ibar and about the best *kajmak* in the world. Sometimes, over a glass of brandy, Irina's father shed a tear remembering the execution of the Kraljevo high school students.

On a July afternoon in 1990, ten years after Tito's death, Irina's parents visited us in my mother's small apartment next to the School of Law. Apricot brandy was served. Irina's father became exuberant. My mother laughed like an actress. Irina's mother pursed her lips. I kept Irina company in the sweltering kitched with the blinds drawn. Irina arranged cobalt cups on a tray.

"Open a box of *Jaffa* cookies for me, please" she said.

I refused to help her. I was just hanging out in the kitchen breathing down her neck.

"Stop it," Irina laughed. "You're not helping so get out."

With a coffee spoon, Irina put a little froth into each cup. She arranged the cookies and the spoons on the tray, which made the cobalt set clink, and took it towards the living room. Now I'll tell you what I've been longing to tell you all the time: Irina wore a breezy summer dress. I imagined rather than saw the lines of her panties underneath the dress. I walked a step behind her as she carried the tray to the living room. In the hallway, I put my arm around her waist and grabbed her lower stomach. The cobalt set on the tray shivered.

"Are you crazy?" Irina gasped. Something in her voice moved me. That wasn't a real refusal. In the living room, separated by the frosted glass door, our parents were engrossed in conversation.

"Hey, what are you two doing in there," Irina's father shouted indifferently behind the glass. "Where's that coffee?"

Irina's hands were busy holding the tray. At first I wasn't serious when I pressed myself against Irina from behind in the darkened hallway. I tried to take her panties off and they unexpectedly dropped down to her knees.

"What's wrong with you," she asked in a whisper in which there was more passion than respect for those behind the glass.

I unbuttoned my pants and wedged my aching member between her thighs. I discovered that Irina was quite ready so I slipped into her.

"I'm crazy," I thought.

"You're crazy," whispered Irina echoing my thoughts.

Irina still held the tray while her dress was lifted and her panties hung at her knees. I started to slowly rock pulling her to me and bouncing off her elastic buns. The cups on the tray responded with a fine jingle. In the living room, separated by the frosty glass, our parents were intoxicated by their conversation about the Serbs being the oldest nation in the world and the Cyrillic alphabet being much more beautiful than the Roman alphabet. Then Irina's father started to talk about something really interesting:

"After the war, as a young officer, I often went to Pančevo. There were a lot of orphans from Kordun there. There were teenage girls who would fall in love, but we officers didn't care that much."

"I wouldn't bet on that," I thought as I pulled Irina to me while she was holding the tray. Irina was submissive. Luscious. Fantastic. The cups on the tray jingled as I rebounded from her firm butt. Irina lifted her hips, passionately rolling her head. Farmers would call that "bucking." It was like a dream. She was like a dream.

"So we would come to a dance in the evening," in a good mood, Irina's father continued with his story in the living room. "The orphaned teenage girls arrived at the dance in white blouses and calico skirts. The atmosphere was a combination of poverty and gala. The music started and, slowly, so did the dance. And then, suddenly, one of those gals collapsed on the floor, twisted her neck, and kicked her feet: Airplanes! Airplanes! – she shouted. All of a sudden, a dozen kids were kicking their feet and foaming at the mouth on the floor. In a fit of mass hysteria, the epileptics shouted: Airplanes! – or raved about the *ustashe*. In the silent dance hall, those kids in white blouses were flopping on the parquet like fish."

Half drunk, Čedomir wiped away a tear from the corner of his eye and concluded:

"That's what trauma is, my friends. Yugoslav communist authorities bribed people into forgetting those things. Now the money is spent, communism is gone, while the traumas are emerging from amnesia."

I enjoyed feeling Irina's slipperiness with my aroused member. I was pulling her to me and bouncing away from her firm hemispheres.

"Oh, how I'm fucking her!" I thought.

"Oh, how he's fucking me!" she thought.

Irina's desire fueled my desire. The best sex of the Millennium was taking place in Belgrade, almost in the presence of our parents, in a small apartment next to the School of Law. What can I compare that experience with? At first the lips mechanically repeat a prayer, and then God's presence fills the one praying. After the moment of sexual mechanics – from the universe, from heaven and earth, from everywhere, there rushed a sudden tide of ultimate pleasure that engulfed and filled both Irina and me. That's how Adam and Eve fucked before their expulsion from Eden.

"Trauma is a horrible thing," in a funereal voice, Irina's mother spoke for the first time that afternoon. "In Neimar, we had a neighbor named Novica, a plumber. Whenever something broke down in our house, he came to fix it. He charged peanuts for his services. He was the quietest and the best man ever. He was a Serbian orphan who survived *ustashe* massacres in Banija..."

While Dafina was talking in the next room, the cobalt cups jingled on the tray which Irina still held onto desperately. She wasn't pretending anymore. She rolled her head like a reined in mare. I sucked on her neck, grabbing her breasts with one hand and her hip with the other. The cups jingled. The tide was coming.

"During communism, Novica's memories were frozen," Irina's mother continued in a throaty voice. "When the televised campaign of hatred started, when they started digging up the bones of slaughtered Serbs from World War II from the pits, Novica's buried memories came back. He went to the bathroom and hanged himself."

In the living room, flanked by two concerned women, Čedomir wiped away a tear as he realized that, in Yugoslavia, World War II traumas found their way back from amnesia.

With all the power in my toes and calves, I thrusted myself forward. Irina violently bent herself backwards. What a bitch! – my thoughts went crazy. The rosy cloud of eroticism which up until then floated above my shoulder suddenly entered my hips and Irina's entire body and flooded both of us. The tide of shining light and liquid gold engulfed our senses... Yes, the tide engulfed us! With my left hand, I grabbed Irina's upper arm. I thrusted the fingers of my right hand into her crotch.

At long last, Irina dropped the tray and it hit the floor like a gong. The coffee splattered. The cookies rolled over the floor. The precious cobalt set shattered to pieces. Like fleas, the shards hopped to the farthest corners of the hallway.

CHAPTER 14

A tale of a knight

How can I write about a fragmented life other than in fragments?

In my childhood, a tale of a knight made the deepest impression on me. I don't remember the knight's name nor why they wanted to draw and quarter him. Should I say that the story first fired my imagination when I read Ripley's "Believe It or Not" in the children's weekly *Politikin Zabavnik*? The knight was lying in the middle of the square of the town that could have been Aachen or Carcassonne. The ropes that cut into his legs and arms were tied to four sturdy black horses. Hungry stray dogs were yawning in the square. The henchmen whipped the horses expecting each of them to pull away a leg or an arm. That didn't happen.

The knight was a man of extraordinary strength. When the ropes became taut and lifted him from the ground, he flexed his arms and legs and the core of his life – his belly. The black horses started to slip on the wet cobblestones. With the strength of his body, the crucified man succeeded in pulling the horses back. The crowd gasped as one. The henchmen and the judges put their heads together deliberating what to do. The knight stared at the sky as he waited for their decision.

The head henchman pulled back his hood and nodded for them to go on with the execution. The black horses were whipped again. The taut ropes lifted the knight off the ground. All his muscles constricted into a single knot. With a scream that came from the utmost depth of his being, he pulled his arms and legs towards his navel. The horses stumbled backwards. The crowd was drunk with disbelief: Nothing like that had ever happened before. The judges withdrew for a short consultation and decided to continue with the execution.

A crack of the whip sounded and the horses' haunches swayed. Each black horse strained to pull away a part of the knight's body. The knight's muscles turned into stone from effort. Each fiber stretched to the breaking point. The knight's joints bent inwards. The horses snorted nervously. Their hooves slipped in place. The third gasp from the crowd was stronger than the previous two. The henchmen and the judges yelled: A miracle! After three attempts to execute him, they decided to grant the knight his life.

I am that knight.

Different parts of my life – my mind and my desires, various experiences and observations – rush each in its own direction in an attempt to pull me apart. Each piece of the mosaic of my life is a horse. I resist, pulling them back towards my navel. I try to stay whole. I hope that, due to my desperate efforts, they will grant me my life. The effort I'm talking about is this book.

CHAPTER 15

"The blind say that the eyes stink"
(a saying from Cameroon)

A Blind Man

In the last decade of the Millennium, in 1991 to be exact, the world definitely shattered into fragments. Zora told us how a blind man passed her in a rush furiously tapping his white cane in the street. She wondered aloud if Belgrade turned into a city of rushing blind men.

Boris gave her a dark look.

Sybil's Prophecies

It was the year 1991.

It was the year 7486 of the Alexandrian calendar.

It was the year 1369 according to the Hijrah.

It was the 202nd year after the French Revolution.

It was the year of the Goat in the Chinese calendar.

That year Yugoslavia fell apart. Belgrade's ruler Tarquin the Proud refused to buy Sybil's prophecies, so she burned them. In the society in which I lived, Tarquin the Proud set the ruling norm based on inane wickedness combined with aimless cunning.

The more of a conniving jerk one was, the more appreciated he was at the court of Tarquin the Proud. They would say: He's smart. The more of a brazen maniac one was, the more appreciated he was. They would say: He's enterprising. The more of a primitive idiot one was, the more appreciated he was. They would say: He's authentic. In the early 1990s, such smart, enterprising, and authentic people lived at the court of Tarquin the Proud.

This is how Tarquin the Proud ruled: He started talking about the importance of the ashtray. Then he broke the ashtray and started talking about the exceptional usefulness of the chair. Then he broke the chair and started talking about how we can't live without clothes. Then he tore up the clothes and started talking about the key importance of the carpet. Then... Then nothing. People admired the carpet, having forgotten the ashtray, the chair, and the clothes. It was easy for Tarquin the Proud to rule the people over whom the Millennium cast a shadow, leaving them mute and without memories.

The Tanks

On the 9th of March, 1991, in Belgrade armored policemen looked like a black row of Grendels behind their translucent shields. The mob showered them with cobble-stones. As a symbol of that day, a woman fearlessly stood in the jet of a fire hose. I experienced claustrophobia and suffocation from tear gas. Out of breath, Irina told me:

"Zora and I just sat down and ordered cokes when the tanks entered the Terazije Square."

Foundations shook, Belgrade was shattered by the tanks' entrance.

All over Yugoslavia, barricades were put up and torn down around its cities. The evil grew. It grew ever worse and ever more shameful. The first man, I remember, was killed at a soccer match. After that, I don't remember the exact order of deaths.

One day, my TV set said: Dear viewers, Yugoslavia has been experiencing the most dramatic moments since World War II. People whispered: Treason! The radio called for a mobilization. The media intoxicated people like nerve gas. Various regular and breaking news were broadcasted day in and day out. Belgrade TV asserted that Austrian soldiers fought arm in arm with Slovene territorials. The Slovene media claimed that the regular Yugoslav army was committing heinous atrocities in Slovenia. The mothers who didn't know where their soldier-kids were, broke into the Assembly Building. The TV broadcasted their blabbering.

And so on. And so on... And so on...

The Praise of Folly

To the question of what caused the war in Yugoslavia, my pat response is that each Yugoslav family used to have a rabid fascist in their living room. It was their TV set.

Folly addressed the citizens of Yugoslavia from the screen and called for war. When Folly issued the call, people laughed and applauded. Faces beamed with fresh and uncontrollable joy. Furrowed brows became smooth. Moody and dejected people smiled the smiles of hope. Erasmus of Rotterdam taught that there is no special glory in war and the courage of the tough guys who wage it is inversely proportional to their brains. Erasmus repeatedly said that the glorious game of war is played by parasites, thieves, murderers, dullards, pimps, drunks and generally other dregs of mankind. To the power that calls for war, Erasmus gave the name Folly and pointed out that its nurse maids were Drunkenness and Ignorance. But now and forever, that power pretends to be the very spirit of youth and asserts that, like spring, it endows everything with a different hue.

The Soul

In the environment in which I lived, love became much more shameful than hate. And all those barking mountain baboons were in the right as they relied on their "natural" hatred, while my "artificial" love – as a Croatian writer friend of mine called it – had no supporting points at all. Generally speaking, the soul is home-less. In the movie *After Midnight*, a black musician says: "A fish is in the ocean, a child is in his mother, and the soul is in the void." It really is in the void.

Voices

I had a bad dream. In the dream, my father and my mother emotionally told me:
"Dear son, be an asshole!"
The representatives of my *alma mater* told me:
"As a representative of the intellectual elite, be an asshole!"
The emissaries of the military and the police told me:
"Honorable patriot, be an asshole!"
My girlfriend Irina cuddled with me and, with the tip of her tongue, slipped the words into my ear:
"Sweetheart, be an asshole!"
I tore off my pajamas a moment before I suffocated.

Medea

I watched *Medea* on TV.
The nurse said: "Life is better than death."
Medea said: "Not now!"

Hunger

On the radio the rock band *Catherine the Great* sang: "Hunger is stronger than any truth."

The Roosters

In the last decade of the Millennium, the ground opened up beneath us and we dropped down to fifty years before, right into the jaws of World War II. I read that an entire village in Montenegro was swallowed up by a tectonic disaster. For a couple of mornings after that, roosters could still be heard crowing from underneath the ground. Those roosters crowing from under the ground reminded me of us.

The Eyes

In an effort to explain what happened to us, I'll tell you a Czech fairy tale in which the bloody setting illustrates the circumstances in which I lived. In the tale, forest fairies Yezinkas gouged an old shepherd's eyes. A boy hoodwinked the fairies and tied them up thus forcing them to return the sight to the old man (it's no accident that an old man lost his sight while a boy is returning it to him). The fairies took the boy to their cave and showed him a pile of eyes in the corner. The boy chose a pair and placed them back in his old friend's sockets, but the shepherd wailed: "Oh, those aren't mine, owls are the only thing I can see." The boy offered him another pair from the pile, and the old man complained: "These aren't mine either, I can only see wolves."

Before I finish the tale, I have to pause and whisper a few words in our defense. If the name of a people from this part of the Balkans – especially the people I belong to – at one point could become a synonym for murderers, don't forget they were eyeless, in a world without a supporting point or law. In their darkness, someone else's eyes were offered to them. With one pair, they saw only conspiracies. With the other pair – only murderers. I pray to God to give us one more chance, to allow us to choose again from that horrible pile, to help us find real eyes, those that can take in a different perspective, so that – like the hero of the tale – we can sigh with relief:

"These are mine. Thank God, now I can see well again."

CHAPTER 16

The tale of a cannibal

The countdown to the Millennium was in progress. With each moment, we kept sinking into the quicksand. First the war in Slovenia sucked us down. Then the war in Croatia pulled us even deeper.

"How strange life is," Bane murmured.

We were tasting apricot brandy at Boris' friend Milenko's in Surčin. We were sitting in the cement courtyard of a farm house. It was the summer of 1991. The pig pens stank. There was an opera on the old radio. Alfredo from *La Traviata* was singing about love – mysterious and powerful – the circulatory system of the universe. Zora absentmindedly stared at the pale orange reflection of the sun on the cement. I enjoyed the sunset, drank apricot brandy, and exchanged glances with Irina.

"This is a glorious moment," Irina said. "Stench! Opera! Pig pens!"

"Life!" I proudly concluded.

Zora came back from her thoughts and suddenly said:

"Yesterday at the Kalenić Market I saw a cannibal."

"What cannibal?"

"The cannibal was a woman in a dress with large flowers who bought a piglet at a cheap price," Zora said. "They caught the piglet in the war in Slavonia where dead bodies litter the cornfields. The piglet ate the dead bodies there. It ate Kurds. It ate *zengas*[1]. – Ha, ha. It grew fat – the cannibal woman laughed with glee. – Now we're going to wolf it down!"

---

1   "Kurdish mercenaries were believed to have fought alongside the Croats in the Yugoslav civil war; *zengas* were members of the Croatian paramilitary units."

"Get out of here, woman, I'm sick of you," an old man told her.

"The cannibal didn't react," Zora continued. "With her big lips and large tits she remained completely unruffled. She laughed and her gold tooth reflected light. Now it was her turn to eat the pig that ate people. She guffawed. I saw a cannibal."

Boris frowned:

"One shouldn't talk about certain things even… if… we come across them."

"That cannibal ought to be fucked," drunken Bane shouted. "A quart of sperm should be poured into her. The big lips, the large tits, and the particularly arousing erotic detail – the gold tooth. Big lips. Big tits. A cannibal."

Love – mysterious and powerful!!! – Alfredo was singing.

The pig pens stank ecstatically.

CHAPTER 17

A tale of a beauty

"So you saw a cannibal in our town," Boris told Zora. "And I saw a beauty."

"What beauty?" Zora asked.

"I saw her once before at the printing shop of the *Glas* behind the Assembly Building and I have never forgotten her. I was struck dumb when that woman entered. She wasn't young anymore but there was no doubt she personified what poets call eternal beauty. She had silvery hair and eyes that flashed with light. I regret I didn't approach that elderly woman and tell her: You're awfully beautiful. Whispering, I asked my friend, the layout manager, about her. – Ah – the wild-haired bohemian sighed. – If you only knew what kind of woman she was. Both the truly great ones and the great wannabes courted her. She ignored them. She followed her own way. She never married. She's very sick now.

I visited the layout manager again last week. I saw the beauty again. With her elegant profile, she resembled the Egyptian holy cat. I couldn't believe my eyes – she was already an old woman! For the first time, I noticed she limped. She walked supporting herself with a cane to which my imagination added a silver handle. She looked like a Russian countess in a Davos sanatorium. I observed her elongated profile and enjoyed the glint of her green eyes and silvery hair. There was something indestructible in that woman's beauty. She possessed a shard of immortality. I must say this woman is still an ornament of Belgrade. Nothing – neither old age nor illness, not even the last gasp of breath can erase the stamp of astounding beauty from one such face."

CHAPTER 18

Tales from the zoo

Ships full of weapons kept coming to the country from everywhere. Around Bosnian cities, barricades appeared and then disappeared. On the screen, TV prophets went amok. Belgradians stood in line to invest their money in bank pyramid-schemes. Caligula's horses neighed in the National Assembly. And what did we do? Like those who tried to flee the plague in Florence, we told tales to each other. Only that now no one had time for the whole tale. In our *Decameron* it was enough to briefly sketch out someone's life story or mention a telling detail at least.

Who said that God is in the details?

Who said that things ceased to exist in a chronological and linear way and began to follow mosaic-like and simultaneous patterns?

Who said that the truth evades a methodical person?

***

"People in our beautiful city began to get on my nerves, so I started to go to the Kalemegdan Zoo," I told my tale to Zora, Boris, Bane and Irina. "I strolled among the animals and watched gold, silver and ordinary peacocks. I watched inflamed simian asses. I watched an elephant rocking forward and backward in despair. I watched arrogant llamas and giraffes with long eye lashes. I also watched people who go there.

At the zoo, I ran across a family of unkempt yokels who went from cage to cage in awe. To the yokel family members, the animals were something new. They watched them with a lot of hatred. The motionless crocodile looked like a piece of wood. That annoyed them, so they tried to make it move throwing coins at it. Then the unkempt yokel kid ran up to the pool where a seal twirled in the azure water like a flash. The kid bared his teeth and yelled: Look! A frog!

The father came up to the pool. He grinned with the same amount of disgust like his son. He fixed his eyes on the black, wet creature and barked: That ain't a frog, that's a hedgehog!"

Irina sneered:

"That ain't a frog, that's a hedgehog?! That'll be our inside joke."

I raised my hand to let them know that I wasn't finished:

"The same day at the zoo I came across people who patted tigers. I saw a woman in a sunflower dress who approached the cage containing five supple tigers. A younger man videotaped her. The woman came up to the cage and stuck her arm through the bars. I flinched and closed my eyes: Now the tiger will bite her hand off. But nothing happened. I opened my eyes. I saw a huge tigress rubbing herself against the extended hand. The woman cooed: My little one. My sweetie.

The cage with tigers is placed on the corner of the Kalemegdan fortress. A man with an umbrella walked by on top of the fortress wall. The tigress became agitated. The old broad in the sunflower dress cooed rapidly: C'mon, Kali, my girl. No one's gonna hurt you. Mommy's here. Calm down.

What in the world is this, I thought. What city am I in? What planet? Where can you find an old broad patting the Indian goddess of death to calm her down? Then I remembered that the Belgrade Zoo was recently short of funds for milk and gave away cubs to volunteers who raised them at home. So this enormous tigress grew up at the home of the woman in the sunflower dress."

"But that's not the weirdest thing in your story," Irina noticed. "The weirdest thing is that the most glorious and strongest creature in the world, the tigress Kali, was afraid of something and that her Belgrade step mother had to comfort her."

"Yes," I responded looking Irina straight in the eyes. "If Kali was afraid of something, then everyone is. All the creatures in the world. Gorgeous women. Tigers. Everyone except God."

CHAPTER 19

The smell of the leopard

"I have a cocker spaniel, Mimi, whom I love a lot," Zora smiled warmly. "Mimi is a sweet but dumb puppy. All he knows about the wide world is the deep carpet in the living room and the kitchen floor where his food awaits him daily. Last week I took Mimi for a walk in Tašmajdan Park. I didn't know that the Belgrade Zoo gave away some cubs to people to foster in their apartments and feed them milk till they grow up. One of the ladies who adopted a cub from the zoo walked her little leopard in Tašmajdan Park at the same time."

"Of course, my Mimi didn't have a clue what a leopard was," Zora cleared her throat emphatically. "To tell you the truth, the baby leopard looked like a cat, and one might suppose Mimi would chase it. Mimi didn't chase it. Even before he saw it, he caught the smell of the leopard and panicked. Contrary to what sociologists tell us, it's obvious that some information exists outside of experience. The smell of the leopard made a domesticated dog like my Mimi go berserk. When a dog is unsure whether to fight or run, it starts to limp. Mimi started to limp. Then he started to tremble and couldn't calm down till I carried him back home."

"That's what I've been telling you all the time," Boris triumphantly cut in. "In this day and age, we're all like Zora's cocker spaniel Mimi. We've all caught the smell of the leopard. We've caught a threatening smell, deeper than our own experience, and each of us is limping, unsure whether to fight or to run."

Bane gazed into the distance with his steppe-like eyes and said:

"How strange life is."

CHAPTER 20

In which Death and Madness brush shoulders with Bane Janović

Everything that happened to us first appeared on TV and then in life. Television didn't reflect events – it created them. First on the screen, then in reality, everything went through a Bruegel--Bosch like distortion. Some deacon tapped a child's skull with his pencil in the TV studio. People whom God sculpted with his toes debated on the screen. One political representative talked about how he once fished using dynamite and another how he once wrestled a bear.

"I don't want to think about them. I don't want to know their names. I don't want to associate with scum," Bane yelled.

"Grow up," Boris said softly. "They can draft you and you can't draft them."

That's exactly what happened.

Before he got drafted, Bane Janović held a series of concerts called *Photogenic Thoughts*. On the tour, he apologized to girls for being "polyamorous." What did the word polyamorous mean? It meant that Bane was unable to be with only one woman at a time. My friend seriously expounded on his diagnosis to girls as if he talked about diabetes. Girls believed him. To me Bane defined the same problem in simpler terms:

"I can't live without pussy."

Whenever he talked with the saxophone player Marija on the phone, Bane closed his eyes. He still had a toothbrush in her apartment. In addition to his old love, he had two other lovers. Neda was ten years younger and called him "a dirty old man." Tanja was ten years older and called him "my boy." Bane was at the cross-roads. He still didn't know whether he should go to his mother's in America or stay in Belgrade. When he thought he would go, he embraced the maliciously dull solipsism: "Everything here is re-pugnant because it's repugnant, and it's repugnant because everything is repugnant."

"Why don't you go?" I wondered. "I'd go, but I don't have a place to go. All the doors are closed to me. No one opens their arms to greet me anywhere."

"Why should I go there?" Bane's answer shocked me. "They don't sing the same songs there."

"I don't get Bane," I told Boris many times.

"He's bullshitting," Boris responded laconically.

Zora Stefanović encouraged Bane to emigrate. If she were a guy, she said, no way she would go to war. This was due to her con-viction, currently embraced by an absolute minority, that Croats and Serbs were the same people.

"If someone attacked Croatia, I would go, but I wouldn't go against Croatia," she stated her opinion with a straight face.

"Since you're not a guy, your argument is null and void," Ba-ne responded.

One ugly day, history knocked on Bane's door in the form of a draft officer. It was a very unusual draft situation. In Belgrade, the majority of people went into hiding and slept in their friends' apartments. Mothers wept over the coffins of the sons who went to war and died. But nothing happened to those who refused to go. I remember that the days were so hot that our thinking became fuzzy. Bane filled the tub with cold water and slipped into it hug-ging a watermelon which was getting cooled. That's when he heard the doorbell. He opened the door wrapped in a towel while water dripped on the rug. That's how he received the draft summons.

History will never again knock on Bane Janović's door and say: "I'm sorry I ruined your life." I don't understand why a rock musician, who scoffed at the world, answered a draft summons. Only a few days earlier, Bane insisted that our beloved leaders regressed from fools to madmen and that we could only hope that one day they would evolve back into fools. Why did Bane go to war? More than once I've noticed that our people who scoff at the world like anarchists deep down have a high regard for authority. The idiotic respect for authority somehow stirred in Bane. Like a dutiful citizen (I can barely suppress a giggle at the thought of Bane as a dutiful citizen!), he responded to the call! I assume that a dutiful citizen of a savage society like the Aztec's calmly took part in ripping out a thousand human hearts. Bane's older girlfriend Tanja was Croatian. She squeezed his hand as they parted and looked at him with teary eyes.

"Why are you staring at me with such an anguished, religious gaze?" Bane asked as his own eyes filled with tears.

They sent Bane to Slavonija where the pig from Zora's story got fat on corpses. There people from Valjevo in Serbia and Vinkovci in Croatia, who wept together at Tito's funeral ten years before, now tried to kill each other. The portable radios of both Serbs and Croats blasted the music of *Azra*:

> ... *sons of bitches,*
> *mannequins of blood, without a speck of brain,*
> *murderers on the road...*

Those were ugly, bloody, lousy times. The times of fear, shame, and rage. The slaughter, destruction and looting around Vukovar dragged on for a long time. At night, the tracers cut the air. Tanja constantly prayed for Bane to be spared. He told me that at times unbearable fear descended on him in the dark:

"All of a sudden, a fuse lights up in your head, so you have to open fire."

This is what he had to say about the officers:

"I've never seen such a collection of vermin in my life. You could curse them, do whatever you wanted to them. It was fine. All you had to do was show up. Captain Ristić shut himself in a house he refused to leave. He gave his orders through the window."

As he sneered at Ristić, Bane made friends with Mile Protić, a bug-eyed drunk from Ub.

"Too much water won't make you drunk but it might make you drown," Protić offered Bane some brandy. Then he took a swig and continued to philosophize: "Drink or don't drink, you'll wind up six feet under. That's the only justice. Otherwise, *they*," Protić winked and vaguely gestured referring to everyone who was in command in this world, "would live three hundred years, like mammoths. But the way things are – uh-uh! Six feet under! And the sound of the bugle playing *Taps*…"

Mile Protić couldn't get serious no matter what he talked about. His habitual smile flickered across his face as he spoke to Bane:

"The only thing I can't forgive my mother for is… bringing me into the world…"

When Protić was killed by a sniper, Bane drank a whole bottle for the soul. He kept on getting wasted worse than Protić as he observed criminals – the avant-garde of war – running amok. They threatened to lock him up in a pig pen in Erdut. Bane watched cornfields set ablaze; the burning corpses stank ecstatically. He was amused by the story of a soldier who went from the front lines right to downtown Belgrade in a tank. But in the very next moment, fear – piercing as the sound of a dentist drill – nested in Bane's soul. That was the time of limping dogs, when it was difficult to keep a level head. Bane's hero was the young man who killed himself as he sat indecisively between two groups of reservists from Valjevo – one that stayed on the front lines and the other that "deserted" and went back home, not knowing what they were fighting for. How many people, Bane wondered, faced with the dilemma between moral and physical death, would choose the physical.

On the left was day, on the right was night. The choice was life or death.

Bane buried his head in his hands and growled:

"Disgusting. Disgusting. Disgusting."

"I thought I was going crazy," he said to me later on.

"If I were you, I wouldn't have responded to the call in the first place. And in the second, I would have acted crazy from the start."

"All my instincts lied to me," Bane wept. "I was absolutely certain that I would get killed. I had no doubt about it. They sent me for an observation. I didn't even pretend, believe me."

As early as his boot camp experience in Bubanj Potok, my friend showed signs of instability. After Protić's death, Bane ended up under observation at a military mental hospital. That young man, who once straightened himself up on the flood-lit stage like a god and controlled the bodies of the dancing masses, now lay scrunched in the fetal position under a gray blanket. Sometimes Bane managed to read in the hospital. An excerpt from Rebecca West's *Black Lamb and Gray Falcon* hit Bane with the power of prophesy. That excerpt from the description of a Mostar hotel read as follows:

"Young officers moved rhythmically through the beams of white light that poured down upon the acid green of the billiard-tables, and the billiard balls gave out their sound of stoical shock. There was immanent the Balkan feeling of a shiftless yet just doom. It seemed possible that someone might come into the room, perhaps a man who would hang up his fez, and explain, in terms just comprehensible enough to make it certain they were not nonsensical, that all the people at the tables must stay there until the two officers who were playing billiards at that moment had played a million games, and that by the result their eternal fates would be decided; and that this would be accepted, and people would sit there quietly waiting and reading the newspapers."

That's exactly what happened.

In the last decade of the Millennium, the devil entered our lives and ordered us not to move. The officers from Rebecca West's prophecy, played their one million games of billiards. And in the military asylum, Bane Janović awaited the verdict regarding his fate. He lay on a metal bunk. Between whitewashed walls. Behind the window protected with metal wire. Tears ran down his cheeks while he told me about that:

"That's when I vowed," Bane growled through his whimpering, "that I'd leave the country if I made it out alive."

CHAPTER 21

On Jonah and Daniel

When Bane Janović took a walk around Belgrade after the war, the city looked unreal to him. The returning veteran wondered how people could mistake this civilian mirage for life. After the Slavonijan mud, Belgrade appeared gloriously beautiful. People weren't dressed in uniforms but in a variety of quality apparel. Wherever he went, Bane noticed soldiers whom other Belgradians ignored. To his mother, who regularly called from New York, he said that he met with a psychiatrist once a week. He complained that the sedatives he was taking turned him into a zombie. When he returned to Belgrade, he stopped playing music and seeing girls. Daily walks by the river calmed him down.

One Sunday, as usual, Bane inhaled the smell of silt as he strolled between the confluence of the Sava and the Danube and the restaurant *Venice* in Zemun. God scattered seagulls like confetti above the Danube. Bane first looked for a long time at the prongs of the seagulls' wings. Then he stared at the sand, licked smooth by the waves. The day was warm, so he took off his shoes and socks. His bare feet sank in the sand as he walked towards the river. Bane squatted in the shallows to rinse his hands. He was thinking of his psychiatrist: How much did that old man, who smoked three packs of cigarettes a day, really know? How much did he care about helping him? Could he, dear God, help him at all?

As he squatted in the shallows, lost in thought, a wave splashed over his knees. Bane raised his eyes. He thought a tug boat was passing by, pushing three barges from Russia. He was still thinking about his psychiatrist. How much real understanding and human empathy did he have behind his professional manner? At that moment, a large wave splashed over Bane's head and knocked him on his ass in the mud.

"What the...," Bane opened his mouth and water filled it.

Bane couldn't figure out where a muffled, omnipresent sound was coming from. It appeared that the entire universe echoed with the threatening rhythm: "Ba-bump! Ba-bump! Ba-bump!"

"Shit," Bane growled spitting out the muddy water. With an enormous hiss, the Danube parted before him. A whale gaped at Bane aiming to swallow him. The whale was completely white, the biggest whale in the world. Bane knew it was Moby Dick, the monster that resides in the rivers and oceans of all countries. The previous week, it might have been in Australia or Africa, but today it caught Bane in the Danube. He realized that the muffled "ba-bump," "ba-bump," "ba-bump" sound was the beating of the whale's heart under the water. The monster's gullet, resembling an underwater cave, reeked of iodine and algae. The whale sucked in air and swallowed Bane Janović...

The whale dove. The young man in its stomach heard how, outside, the water swooshed with the power of Victoria Falls. Bane despaired because he was aware that the whale swam towards the Black Sea and then farther on towards the Atlantic. He wept in the fetid gut of the whale that carried him away from the place of his birth and toward some unknown, glacier-cold regions. Bane was like Jonah, the son of Amitai, who cried from the whale's stomach. Kelp dragged across his face. The depths were around him, and the flood surrounded his soul. Bane remembered God and addressed Him with the words:

"Oh, Jehovah, if your ears don't reach to the depths, where then shall we go? To whom shall we plead? Oh, Jehovah! Have your waves closed above my head forever?"

Bane's sense of smell was faster than his eyes which couldn't penetrate the darkness of the whale's stomach. Through the stench of algae, he caught a whiff of the musky odor of a beast. Bane's ears woke up in the dark. He first heard the sound of a cat-like movement in the whale's stomach. Then he heard a muffled growl. After that, a large body brushed against his hip. Bane stuck his hand over his mouth to stifle a cry. He pulled a lighter out of his pocket. The flame soundlessly sprouted above the polished surface of the lighter.

"If that didn't make me faint, nothing will," Bane wrote to me later.

The cave he was in was full of floppy-eared lionesses and handsomely-maned lions. The white whale must have swallowed them earlier, somewhere in Africa. In the flickering light of the flame, the lions moved like sand and mated ten times in a row. Bane dropped the lighter and burned his fingers. That was the signal for the lions to start roaring. Dear mother! Lord creator! Whoever hasn't heard lions roaring from up close can't imagine what Bane experienced. It seemed to him that the sound permeated each and every pore of existence. It seemed that it came from everywhere even from within himself. Bane couldn't hope that his prayer would overpower the roaring of the lions. And yet, he started to pray.

"... Because you are my lamp, oh Jehovah, you will light up my darkness," he whispered among the roaring lions.

Bane Janović was like Daniel who believed the lions would grind his bones into powder, in the rocky cave that King Darius sealed. Bane was both Jonah and Daniel. He prayed in the lion's den which was also the whale's stomach. He whispered that the nets of death had fallen over him and that Jehovah was his fortress. For three days and three nights he prayed deep under the sea while the lions roared around him and mated fifty times in a row. Bane's prayer was just a whisper drowned by the lions' roar but in His halls, the Lord heard him. The foundation of heaven creaked and the earth shook. The Lord addressed the fish-whale. And the white whale surfaced and vomited Bane from his stomach full of algae and the stench of lions onto the dry land. As soon as it spat Bane out, the whale turned quickly around and swam off to swallow some people in China and take them to the same place it took Bane.

When the monster freed him, Bane turned around and saw another monster. He saw a giantess with a crown of spikes and a torch of stone. He realized that it was the Statue of Liberty and that he was on Ellis Island. Across the bay, the glass buildings of Manhattan glowed like glaciers.

The year was 1991.

CHAPTER 22

A discourse on enemies

When I read the letter with the dramatic description of Bane's departure to America, my world shrank. A feeling of desperation grabbed me by the throat. I thought:

"You may have been both Jonah and Daniel, but you got out. But what will happen to me?"

I had a poorly paid job at the Institute for Balkan History. My mother's patients at times expressed their gratitude in money. My mother the doctor supplemented my budget somewhat each month. I was still broke. At the Bajloni Market, I haggled with good natured and not-so-good natured farmers. I dragged bags full of August tomatoes uphill. With the help of my grandfather Teofil, I made tomato sauce, added parsley to it, and poured it into bottles for the winter. In Belgrade's crowded buses, I squeezed myself between old ladies with moustaches. I visited my favorite sites in the city: the island of Međica and the Kosančićev Venac, and I enjoyed the majestic view from Kalemegdan. Belgrade life ran on at its usual pace, in sync with my bloodstream. Sages claim that life – the key to all knowledge – is the most banal of all things. I listened to the sounds of the city I loved… At a table in the *Fresco Café* two young men and a girl had a philosophical discussion about why cigarette smoke always drifts towards the non-smoker. Belgrade women walked braless and our gazes goose-bumped their nipples. One high school student complained to the other: "There are good looking girls, but they are all stuck up." A taxi driver yelled at a truck: "Get going, you damn Pančevo slob, move along!" At the Bajloni Market, a vendor raised a mallet above a carp and asked his customer: "Should I kill it a bit?" A drunk raised his finger in front of the *Restaurant Washington* and shouted out:

"This is Belgrade and even monks marry here!"

Since Bosnia didn't go up in flames right after Croatia, we were hopeful that it never would. The military could still call me up for service. I was still thinking about history. Meša Selimović believed that poetry is an escape from history. I don't know whether that's true or not. No matter how much poetry I read, politicians, newsmen, and diplomats still decided about the course of my life.

News from the numerous reporters on safari in Yugoslavia tended to dramatize the situation rather than understand it. Perhaps most of the reporters would consider the understanding of my own situation as something too personal. None of them asked the key question: What would they do if they were in my shoes? Freud wasn't right. The psychological drive for domination over *the other* is stronger than the sex drive. Yugoslavia provided the raw materials – her own misfortune. Foreign correspondents processed it into a feeling of superiority for themselves and their readers.

A famous Buddhist parable tells about a group of blind men who are trying to describe an elephant. One of them is holding it by the tusk, another by the trunk, a third by the leg, a fourth by the tail. I understand that somebody might feel the calming coolness of ivory in his hand while I'm holding the tail or some other more inappropriate body part. And yet, I'll try to faithfully describe what I felt in my own time.

From the Belgrade perspective, the story of the dissolution of Yugoslavia was the story of the constant loss of points of support. Somebody changed the labels of the bottles in a pharmacy so we couldn't tell the difference between poison and medicine. Everything we used to know didn't work anymore. No matter what pillar of public or private life we leaned on, it started to waver or fell into the blackness of the universe. Living in a world without pillars or points of support, with a diminishing number of friends, I developed a bizarre theory: "One should put one's faith in one's enemies!"

It wasn't the first time that something one loves was vanishing. That's how St. Augustin, the Roman from Africa, must have felt knowing that Rome was to vanish. Augustin had no doubts that the spiritual essence of the empire, Christianity, would survive beyond the structures of the state. The way I felt was much like the way people must have felt at the dissolution of Austria-Hungary. Four artists I loved died with Austria-Hungary in 1918: Gustav Klimt, Egon Schiele, Otto Wagner, and Koloman Moser. I always felt like their progeny even though my country, Serbia, contributed to the downfall of Austria-Hungary. I hope that one day some Albanian writer will continue what I've been doing. In the midst of the bloody breakup of the country in which I lived, I still believed in "the better angels of our nature." Like Pico della Mirandola, I believed man was given the power to determine the limits of his nature on his own. I believe that in the world of Capulets and Montagues, a Romeo and a Juliet can always be born. I believed in the desperate theory, born in the world left without the points of support: One should put one's faith in his enemies!

CHAPTER 23

A melancholy portrait of a traditionalist

"Novalis asserted that everything must occasionally turn into a liquid state in order to go back and resolidify around a solid core. But what are those solid cores?" I asked Zora, Boris, and Irina. "Do you think that those solid cores exist in tradition?"

"Do you know Milan Ocokoljić?" Zora asked in response.

"Sure. He's such an idiot," Boris readily answered.

"Whether he's an idiot or not, the most important thing in his life is…"

"…to continually talk about his rich father," Irina cut in…

"My dad this, my dad that," Boris aped.

"He continually talks about tradition," Irina went on, "and how his family are true Belgradians even though one would ride a horse to death trying to get from Belgrade to his grandfather's village in a day."

"Yeah," Zora smiled. "Me and Milan once went to the island of Medica. We were sitting on the island's tip and watched the water carry clumps of catkins. By the way, I think that the Germans call catkins 'tree snow.' So we watched the water carry that spring snow. The moment was real fine, relaxing. I didn't feel like listening to any crap.

Then Milan again started to talk about tradition, which to him was a synonym for his father and an excuse to brag about him."

Zora's eyes were glowing, like buzzing green flies in August. She waived her hand and interrupted Milan Ocokoljić.

"Enough! Quit harping on it. It's neither good nor healthy to talk about your dad all the time. Let go of your dad."

"Oh God," Zora continued shuddering all over. "*What* a look he gave me. From that look I understood how pathetic the clash between dignity and the need for psychological protection is. Dignity often ends up on the losing side. I realized that Milan uses lies in his battle for self-respect, and that he'll start hating me because I told him that. I realized that it was all over, that his father had broken him and moved into his soul, and that nothing can be done about it. In Milan Ocokoljić's eyes there gaped an abyss of powerlessness and sad finality. Those were the eyes of a man who stepped into a solidifying block of concrete."

CHAPTER 24

St. George on a Dragon Slaying a Horse
– the story of my grandpa

The story about Milan Ocokoljić the traditionalist made me think about my father and my grandpa. I realized I didn't know how to apply the word "tradition" to us. To my father – after World War II and the Revolution – my grandpa's world seemed buried beneath the lava like Pompeii. To me, my father's world looked the same. I've probably become a historian from my desire to remove the layers of petrified lava that separated us and find connections linking the members of my family from the three generations that have been living in Belgrade.

My grandpa Teofil Đorđević was one of the lesser members of the Belgrade Surrealist Movement. In the thirties, Teofil wrote a one-act play called *Limpdick and the Cockstarved Lady*. His wife Jovanka starred in it. Only the director understood the play. To those who ridiculed him as a playwright, Teofil explained that he was, first and foremost, a painter. The wall in our living room was ornamented by a few of his "assemblages" which looked like frozen soup. In the bedroom hung two religious paintings: *St. George on a Dragon Slaying a Horse* and *Christ with Pineapple*. My grandpa's painting that I liked the most was entitled *Squirrels Devouring a Deer*. On the canvas, painted in the Realism manner of Paja Jovanović, a helpless deer was grimacing in agony while bloodthirsty squirrels devoured it alive.

Just before World War II, during his studies in Paris, Teofil Đorđević met the "Pope of Surrealism," André Breton. During his lifetime, he received two letters from Breton. In order to make a "poetic gesture," he wiped his ass with the first one while the second one he had framed and hung on the wall.

Since he knew that French Surrealists granted aristocratic titles to themselves, Teofil Đorđević leafed through a history of Belgrade and chose an aristocratic title that was abandoned in the seventeenth century. The Baroque landowner and the pilgrim by the name of Komnen Georgijević probably was not – but he could have been – Teofil's ancestor. Komnen Georgijević was a Belgradian and the captain of Irig, the lord of Vrdnik, Kukinjaš, and Rivica. His ancestors Hristofor and Laza engaged in clandestine correspondence with the Vienna court as far back as the time of Ferdinand II. Janissaries hung his brother Atanas above a bonfire. Komnen's daughter Marija was taken to the slave market to be sold but managed to escape to Szentendre in Hungary. In the Baroque wars, Georgijević's estates perished together with his mills and his house in Belgrade. The Grand Vizier Köprülü wrote to Komnen in person telling him that all of his possessions would be returned, but nothing came of it. Thus was abandoned the aristocratic title that Teofil Đorđević inherited by his own devices, in the city in which genealogical trees were cut by the sword.

After the son of the wealthy real estate investor Isidor Đorđević had met André Breton, he turned into a communist for a period of time. While the maids licked empty champagne glasses in the Đorđevićs' large apartment, the chaufer would take Teofil to the meetings of the Yugoslav Communist Party. In those meetings, my grandpa would raise his finger and shout: "We must change the world!" As he would return home, he would pause in the foyer before a photograph portraying a man wearing a Serbian peasant hat and a woman with a scarf. Teofil crossed himself before the picture with the caption *The People* and repeated the words of Petar Petrović Njegoš: "Thank you, oh Lord, for elevating me above these common beasts."

During the German occupation of Belgrade, Captain Johan von Noptscha suggested that Teofil Đorđević paint Adolph Hitler's official portraits. Teofil required food rations equal to that of an officer, brushes, paint, and an assistant. After this move, his wife Jovanka informed him that she was leaving him, and that she was taking my father Andrija with her.

Teofil yawned and said:

"Fine, just don't come back and ask me for anything."

In the years between 1941 and 1945 my father Andrija was starving along with the rest of Belgrade, while Grandpa Teofil got plumper and plumper as he painted one Hitler portrait after another. Before those portraits, German soldiers clicked their heels all the way from Hamburg to the Sahara. After the war, Teofil emigrated to London where he worked as a clerk in Mr. Ivanović's shipping company. It took his Surrealist friends fifteen years to convince communist authorities that Teofil was simply a fool, not a real "collaborator." At long last, his friends notified Teofil Đorđević in London:

"You are free to return. You've been forgiven."

In Belgrade, the authorities returned the family apartment next to the Cathedral Church to Teofil.

The first evening in that apartment, my grandpa had a strange dream. He dreamed of bookstores and tea-shops where a man could comfortably grow old. He dreamed of wine-shops organized as neatly as libraries. He dreamed of a town where it was a pleasure to experience the change of seasons. He dreamed of a place that seduced him with details and made him fall in love with the whole. He dreamed of the City constantly built in the dreams of its citizens yet constantly remaining unbuilt.

Teofil's son Andrija soon moved into this Belgrade apartment. Andrija was also a painter. The two painters, the father and the son, had a problem tolerating each other. After they got into a fistfight, they went their separate ways and bad blood remained between them. When Andrija left for Paris, my mother knocked on Teofil's door with a baby in her arms. I have no clue how Milena convinced the Surrealist misanthrope that I was his grandson. The deciding factor, I believe, was that my father sent me presents and that I looked a lot like my grandpa.

When I was eighteen, I moved from my mother's into my grandfather's apartment next to the Cathedral Church, so that I could inherit it one day. His advanced age didn't straighten up the old Surrealist. Even though he was retired, Grandpa still worked part-time for the French division of Radio Yugoslavia and rubbed himself against girls on public transportation. Pushing seventy-five, he retained three priests to give last rites to his male member whom he named Richard Lovejoy. Later he complained that the deceased Dick Lovejoy still haunted him as a vampire.

Teofil sort of liked me in his own way. Sometimes he would pat my head and giggle:

"What an ugly kid!"

At the time when I became obsessed with "adult matters," I asked Teofil whom I saw as a Methuselah:

"Tell me, Grandpa, will this ever let up?"

Teofil's arrogant smile grew warmer. He mussed my hair and said:

"Never."

CHAPTER 25

On my father

During World War II, my father Andrija Đorđević starved while my grandpa Teofil lived in comfort painting the Hitler portraits. Andrija's mother Jovanka, the former actress in the plays that only the director understood, went to surrounding villages and acquired food exchanging her jewelry or pieces of furniture for it. From a man from Surčin, called Dubaja, she bought a slab of bacon for a "gold" watch which in fact was just gilded. After a while, hunger forced her to visit Dubaja again. He complained to her that he lost the watch while fishing. The farmer was unaware of the scam, and so Andrija and Jovanka got some food and were saved for the day. The luck didn't stay with the mother and son for long. Soon, Andrija was forced to steal from German stockpiles. Jovanka died from typhoid fever in Belgrade in September 1944.

Even though Teofil was still around, Andrija lived like an orphan. Half a year he lived on the banks of the Sava where he grew completely wild. He swam in the river at the time when the bodies of the Serbs slaughtered in the Jasenovac concentration camp still floated downstream. Andrija built a tree house on the island of Međica. Many years later, in Paris, he claimed that the mid-stream wooded piece of land always reminded him of Böcklin's *Isle of the Dead.*

When Teofil Đorđević returned to Belgrade, the communist authorities gave him back his apartment next to the Cathedral Church. Faking repentance, Teofil invited his son Andrija to live with him. Because Andrija grew wild during the war, Teofil Đorđević wasn't able to change his son's habit of pissing into the sink. The old man was very careful when it came to politics. He didn't like the fact that a comb could not penetrate the young man's curly beard. Teofil was truly bewildered about what kind of creature his son was. To his old friends, he complained about Andrija:

"A real savage."

My father Andrija Đorđević started to paint during the years of poverty. There were no brushes. No canvas either. Andrija went to the Art Center on Šumatovačka Street to practice drawing. There he learned that well impregnated parchment paper, applied to cardboard or wood, can replace the unattainable canvas. He made his brushes out of the hairs plucked from the inside of a cow's ear. He couldn't forgive his father, whose apartment he moved into, for abandoning him during the difficult war years. The father couldn't forgive Andrija for being a better painter than himself.

"What your son is doing is close to what you Surrealists used to do at one point," an old art critic told Grandpa Teofil.

Those words fell on deaf ears. Teofil and Andrija were both born in the city that was cursed with the generations of sons unable to ever continue the work of their fathers. Between their two generations, a revolutionary volcano erupted, similar to the one that destroyed Pompeii. The lava buried Teofil's world. It was impossible for Teofil and Andrija to recognize mutual similarities. In order to pinpoint a deeper continuity between generations, one needs a historian, which is – let me humbly remind you – my vocation.

"*That* resembles my work?" the former acquaintance of Breton's bristled at the critic's remark. "Never!"

A narcissistic egocentric (my grandpa) and an uncouth savage (my dad) constantly needled each other during the short time they lived together. Teofil bullied his adult son by way of the classical parental repertoire of maltreatment: "How much longer am I going to support you?" or "As long as you live in my apartment, you'll..." Many times the father showed his son the door:

"Get out of my house."

Not being a civilized man, Andrija clenched his jaws in fury. Not wanting to raise his hand against his father, he kicked him in the stomach and moved out. He found shelter with his blind female friend Anja. He slept at her place, or in his tree house on the river island, or in the abandoned German bunkers under the Kalemegdan fortress. Olga told me that he sometimes slept in streetcars. At that time, there were streetcar-shelters that circled around Belgrade all night long. Those after-midnight streetcars were even fitted with a bar where one could have a drink for the road.

In the late fifties there was still a dearth of color and Belgrade was black-and-white. In the black-and-white city, my father noticed a number of beautiful houses that had one thing in common – they weren't his. Weak from hunger, Andrija dragged himself on in a state of daring desperation, filled with déjà vues. He wandered along granite facades looking for shelter to hide in, like a badger before winter.

One day Anja gave him some money, so he got himself a pretzel. In Strahinjić Ban Street he ran into two bums. They both had long beards and white hair that a comb could not penetrate. They were God and St. Peter who wandered upon the earth disguised as beggars.

"Can we have some pretzel," the mysterious beggars asked Andrija. He was first silent, and then he broke off a half and handed it to them. A cat with white socks went by. God touched Andrija and changed the color of his eyes. The touch of God who posed as a beggar made my father the painter he came to be later.

After that encounter, there was a turn for the better for Andrija Đorđević. He first lived with Olga for a short time. Then he lived with my mother for a short time. His last night in Belgrade, Andrija had a dream in which he first founded a city only to abandon it. The next day, he borrowed some money for a ticket and left for France. After ten years of misery, Andrija Đorđević became "our great painter in Paris."

I had little contact with my father the celebrity. Andrija left me behind just like Teofil had left him behind. In between Andrija's time and my time, the volcano of history had erupted again. To me, the Belgrade from my father's time was buried under the lava like Pompeii, and I wouldn't have known anything about it if Olga hadn't told me.

In Paris, my father pretended to despair because his paintings sold for too much. When his countrymen asked him if he was ever a member of the Belgrade art movement *Mediala*, he responded that *Mediala* was peripheral to him. When he was interviewed by the French press, he scrunched his beard and said:

"I like normal people a lot. I'm not normal, but I like normal people."

CHAPTER 26

A trio

It's time to tell you about my first sexual experience. Plotinus was ashamed of having a body. Plotinus was a fool. I'm not ashamed of anything. For my first sexual experience I should thank Bane, who is now in America. When all other boys still lied about their erotic conquests, he told the truth. Since Bane was the first to experience it, he was the first to explain the mysteries of sex to me. For example, he revealed to me a little secret regarding the taste of the cunt: a tad salty, with a touch of iron, finally bland. At the peak of *Kafka's Fiancés'* fame, one afternoon Bane burst into my apartment and urged me to go out with him and "cut loose."

"Where are you taking me?" I asked.

"You'll see!"

Bane's car, an Opel Olympia from 1937, was waiting by the curb. Its tires were two-toned like the shoes of a Cuban gigolo. The seat covers with purple stripes were threadbare. On the dusty hood, someone wrote "Wash me!" The last digit on the speedometer was 120 km/h. If a person put their foot on the fender in order to tie their shoes, the fender would fall off. On the side, the car had a step from which mobsters loved to shoot.

"This car is your best trait," I told Bane.

Bane was an awful driver. He first cussed out the driver of a Golf right in front of him. Then he aimed with his index finger at a woman in the pedestrian crosswalk:

"We're going to run this one over."

"Don't. She's nice."

"She – nice?" Bane was offended.

We parked in front of a semicircular building at the corner of 36 E French Street. There were three wrought iron doors in the entryway. The one on the right led to a watchmaker's shop, the one on the left to the basement, and the middle one, which was locked, to the building. The entryway smelled of life, human longing, and urban poverty. A lantern was hanging from the ceiling, like in a hunter's lodge. A scooter was parked next to a pink marble column.

"This column looks like it's made of mortadella," Bane laughed.

In trepidation, I opened the elevator door fearing to come across one of the monstrosities manufactured by the David Pajić Corp. I was relieved when we entered a nice old elevator with crystal glass and a clear mirror. Noiselessly, it took us to the third floor.

We rang at a dignified-looking door. The door cracked open and a silly-charming eye peered through the crack. The other eye appeared together with a curl of streaked hair. A female face difficult to forget was smiling at us. That was Olga. She ushered us into the living room and turned a switch. A table lamp grew in the light like a mushroom. Standing on lion's claws, pieces of sturdy furniture appeared. The apartment gave me an impression of dizzy depth and knotted complexity. I believed I could step into an armoire and out into the dining room. I was convinced I could step into another armoire and reappear in the roof garden. That's how the apartment seemed to me. My gaze touched every single object in the room we were in. Eventually, I timidly looked Olga in the eye.

The timbre of Olga's voice was moving. She laughed at her own jokes and even her own thoughts. She jingled ice cubes in three glasses and led us into the bedroom. The room was empty except for a couple of double mattresses. Through the shutters, the light of neon signs glided across our bodies as we undressed. There was a fishy smell when she took off her clothes and a musky smell when we took off our underpants.

Olga gently touched Bane's chest, pulled her hand back, and exclaimed, "Oh, my!"

She felt the medal of valor pinned through the bare skin.

"Disgusting," she said.

She carefully pulled the needle out of Bane's nipple and threw the medal on the floor. A trickle of blood spurted from the young man's breast onto the woman's. Olga rubbed Bane's breasts with her breasts and felt mine against her shoulder blades. The wind moved the shutters, and a stripe of light glided over our shoulders. She felt one tongue in her ear and another one in her mouth. Bane and I grabbed each other by the shoulders. In between, Olga gaped like a fish. Three necks rubbed against each other. Slower and slower. Still slower.

Bane turned on his side and obviously fell asleep.

Time eluded me through Olga's nicotine kisses. She kissed my neck and then my chin.

"Do you love me?" I whispered so that Bane couldn't hear me.

She responded in a whisper:

"Do you want me to tell you that I love you?"

My voice stretched out like the arm of a drowning man:

"Yes."

"I love you."

Was the heat I felt on my skin fatigue? Or was it uncertainty? I don't know when I fell asleep, but I know that I dreamed of temples and palaces. I dreamed of well-dressed old men and women, full of life, who were strolling through parks with benches on which lovers intoxicated each other with their breath. I dreamed of sculptures that dotted the squares and the facades of buildings. I dreamed of a thousand restaurants which served the food of a thousand nations. I dreamed of wine-shops organized as neatly as libraries. I dreamed of a city with two rivers that washed its worries away and left it carefree. Then I felt a kiss on one eye, the other eye, the forehead, and finally the lips. She made a sign of the cross over me with kisses.

The first thing I saw that morning was a silly-charming eye and a curl of streaked hair.

"Your smile woke me up," I told Olga. "I felt it through my closed eyelids. Your eyes are so strange. Full of light."

"May good luck follow you on this good morning!" Olga smiled at me.

Bane snuck out and left us alone in the apartment. I took a cup of coffee she offered me, got up, and looked around. A plaster ear was sculpted on a wall of the room.

"Clever," I remarked.

"The wall is eavesdropping," Olga said.

Stark naked, I went out on a small balcony and observed the inner courtyard overgrown with ivy. The old lady-doctor across the way saw me like that.

"Shameful!" she croaked.

I moved away from the balcony. Olga grabbed my upper arm and asked me:

"Look, let's make a deal that what happened last night never happened?"

I really liked her. I asked her:

"If it never happened, how would it be that we met?"

She persisted:

"Let's make a deal that it never happened."

"Fine," I agreed.

She smiled and said:

"It never happened."

Dangling my tool, I walked around the apartment. I nosed around the salon with a nice view of the church. A Secession framework with a silver curvature and a photograph caught my attention. The extremely important photograph eternalized an embracing couple.

Olga was young. She wore bangs and had gray eyes, full of light. Next to her was a young man whose smile crinkled his eyes. He had a beard that a comb could not penetrate.

"Olga!" I shouted. "This is my father in the picture."

"He was the love of my life," Olga said simply.

CHAPTER 27

Frescoes

Before she fell in love with my father, Olga was unhappily married to Čedomir Bojović. After two consecutive miscarriages, Olga fell out of love with her husband. She started going out on her own. Deep voices asked for her on the phone. Since he was fated to become Irina's father, Čedomir put a stop to this unbearable situation. He agreed to the divorce and left his apartment to Olga. Before he got married, Čedomir never washed his socks. Instead, he would throw them away and buy new ones. Even though later I was a frequent guest at their ivy-covered house in Neimar, I never mentioned that I knew about Čedomir's first marriage. The knowledge of that little love secret gave me a sense of power. It amused me to think about the following: If Olga hadn't left Čedomir for my father, Irina wouldn't have ever been born, and if my father hadn't left Olga for the beautiful breasts of my mother, I wouldn't have ever been born. The paths of fate are quite strange.

My father Andrija Đorđević stumbled into Olga's life from the world of bums and stray cats. Before he met Olga, Andrija used to blanket himself with his overcoat, on a box-springs without a mattress, in a drafty attic on Strahinić Ban Street. That kind of life gives one lumbago, bad kidneys, and a curved spine, which turns the person into a question mark with respect to his entire life. Bright-eyed Olga changed the life of the homeless painter Andrija Đorđević as she let him stay in her apartment.

"He wanted to somehow pay me back," Olga pulled me by the arm on the morning I woke up in her apartment on French Street.

She closed the door behind us and announced: "He gave me this room as a gift."

I looked around and said:

"This isn't a room. This is an epoch."

In the apartment on 36 E French Street, I was flabbergasted at a sight of a secular chapel with its walls painted by the great French painter of Serbian origin – my father. In place of Orthodox saints, Andrija Đorđević used symbols that were sacred to him. I examined my father's intimate frescoes with keen attention and a degree of disgust. Sons aren't the best judges of their fathers' work. I will tell you about the impressions those frescoes left me.

1

The way I saw it, the fresco on the first wall represented a primer for understanding all things in this world. The painter obviously craved objects: overcoats, walnuts, protractors, globes, keys, pieces of fabric, retorts, faucets… There were objects found at a dump as well as forgotten objects from the pre-industrial period. The things my father painted hovered in a vacuum, stripped from their functional aspects, just objects in and of themselves. The things shouted: Look at us! The painted objects migrated towards new meanings, like geese in a V. "Everything is nameless," I muttered as I observed the fresco my father painted. "Naming is an act of violence against the world."

Olga held me by the hand and assured me that Andrija touched and licked every single thing he painted. He felt the matter with his fingers, knowing that he would eventually lose it. As he painted, he had a timeless cigarette smoldering in the corner of his mouth. Olga saw her lover Andrija Đorđević as a symbol of the force constantly resisting civilization. To her, my father was "perpetually wild," like an American national park. Olga called him "my Indian" because he painted in the nude and wiped the brushes against his own skin. "I paint carefully," he confided in her, "so it remains interesting even a hundred years from now."

2

On the second wall – at one point the water pipe burst – the surface was bulging. The painter followed the contours suggested by the distortion. He painted the crystallization of some forms and the dissolution of others. In the corners, he painted flying eyes with dragonflies' translucent wings. Right in the middle, he pasted a gaudy old picture frame. Within the frame, he painted Olga "nicely" and "deliberately." That was Olga's portrait in the disintegrating world.

Olga remembered that, during cold days, Andrija wouldn't dress – he only wrapped a blanket around himself and continued to paint. She often found him at the window listening to streetcar bells. During the day, he observed the dome of Alexander Nevsky Church across the street. Throughout the night's silence, he listened to how the sycamores grew. At times, he asked Olga not to come in while he worked. When she finally came in, he would tell her:

"When I'm alone, I see things no one else in Belgrade and in the world can see. I see them because I'm a – monster."

"Okay then, what did you see while you were alone?" Olga asked him.

"A lost day reemerged from the past, and it looked so strange as if it was from the future..." Andrija responded. "A cat on the roof across the street bristled and burst into black smoke... The lights of sleepless windows splashed the black Dorćol buildings. At the same time, butterflies squirmed in their cocoons. With his eyes open, the unborn waited in the womb to be born. A huge spider devoured a dog in the street. God and St. Peter, who strolled through the world, appeared disguised as beggars, and chased the spider away. Then the street sweepers came and hosed off the street. The wet street gave off an angelic scent."

"I didn't know you're a poet," Olga noticed.

"Yes, I'm a poet," Andrija responded and continued to paint.

3

All around the window, Andrija painted the city – a ruin, an enormous public toilet in which every corner and every entryway announced itself with the smell of urine. With bird droppings, Andrija painted the sky above Belgrade's cement courtyards. It was a dead sky, completely anesthetized – looking at it, one couldn't help feeling sleepy. Under that sky, there was the city in all shades of gray. Buildings and city pigeons were of the same color. Everything in that painting looked to be made of the same matter.

"Well, this is a true Dorćol Sunday afternoon," Olga exclaimed when Andrija finished the painting. "The only thing missing is the music of a chanson coming from some window."

"You are clueless," Andrija responded. "You believe things are what we call them, not what they smell like or what they turn into… In this painting, medieval monsters are confronting Renaissance tranquility."

The city Andrija painted looked like cities after the detonation of a neutron bomb. That was a Belgrade of someone who grew up as a stray dog during the occupation and stole coal from German stockpiles. In a seemingly gray world, darkness multiplied darkness, and all blotches grew bigger. From the stillness of a Sunday afternoon in the painting of Andrija Đorđević, some unseen evil threatened. It looked to me that my father's entire work was the expression of an erotic preoccupation with morbidity.

Because...

4

A tremendous absence of innocence hit the viewer from the painting on the fourth wall. It was painted by someone who breathed very slowly. Across the fourth wall of that magic room, there crawled everything we fear or abhor. Surfacing from the painter's memory, dead bodies that the Sava brought from the Jasenovac concentration camp floated there.

The painter ground his teeth at all disgusting things emerging from beneath his brush. He lined up thick, clouded shapes that art critics in Paris would later call "the metaphors of danger and evil." He growled at unbearable things and painted them as such – dangerous and evil. Andrija was elated because *those things* didn't stay inside him. He was on the devil's side, acting like a minor demon, and therefore he believed that the devil would protect him. He believed that the act of painting separated him from what he was painting, and that he only scared and ridiculed the viewers.

"Why are you painting such abominations?" Olga asked him.

"Your ex-husband Čedomir Bojović was a communist and therefore had ideals," Andrija hacked. "He beautified the world. And what did he create? The world that I'm painting!"

I looked at my father's painting on the fourth wall and wondered: Who were the painted creatures with thin arms and spectral bodies? Who were those androgynous angels with rotting mushroom-like heads? Those figures looked like spindly Byzantine fresco corpses decomposing in soap bubbles and turning into swirls of ectoplasm. Disgusting organic forms surrounded them and even intertwined with them. They were like intestines dissolving into soapy foam. Blue-gray and rosy angels had long talons on their toes and idiotic faces. Their swollen faces didn't reveal any interest in their fellow beings.

As soon as he finished, Andrija excitedly showed them to Olga:

"Look how innocent they are!"

CHAPTER 28

The secret history of the Mongols

I asked Olga about my father's friends.

She told me that he was friends with a young man with monstrous glasses who was labelled "a scaled-down Leonardo in our provincial circumstances amidst the dissolution of the modern age"... He was friends with a painter who painted on umbrellas and used manhole covers for prints to create a unique stamp of Belgrade. He was friends with a man who shivered from emaciation like a greyhound and stated:

"The synthesis – the discovery of the crux of the world – is what we are morally obliged to create!"

From the muddy banks of the Sava, my father's friends collected driftwood, "natural sculptures" that the river created. They photographed themselves wearing costumes and a "timeless grimace." They insisted that Belgrade was the hidden navel of the world – just like Bethlehem. On a cheap turntable, they played music full of jungle longing with a hint of chattering tropical birds. On the record – using her enormous range – Yma Sumac sometimes chirped in birds' language and other times growled as if she were possessed.

If one could believe Olga's stories, my father and his friends had their own bench in Kalemegdan Park where they got together after midnight. In the summer, they scaled down the fortress walls and swam over to Great War Island and back. In the fall, they rowed through the fog in stolen boats. In the winter, they snapped icicles from their noses and went to warm themselves in the French Reading Room, *The Russian Tsar*, or *Prešern's Cellar*. They went to the theater of the Film Archives to float for a couple of hours outside of time and space. Black-and-white reflections shimmered over their faces and disappeared inside their open mouths. The wooden theater seats squeaked from their restrained excitement as they watched a movie directed by Vermeer of Delft. At the Film Archives, Eisenstein's hero with glasses shattered by a bullet and starlets from silent movies met them together. The piano spoke for them. From a large poster, Charlie Chaplin winked with his painted eye… From the Film Archives, they went out on the street that was wild with swaying shadows. In the gateway next to the Film Archives, Ingrid Bergman and Humphry Bogart were kissing. In the next gateway, Gerard Philipe and Michele Morgan did the same.

My father and his friends lived in basements – like rats or early Christians – or in attics – like angels or pigeons. At the time when newspapermen were criticized for spreading "pessimism," in the catacombs of communist Belgrade these members of the underground academy read rare books like *The Secret History of the Mongols*. They wrote their own phantom history as well. Altering the world through forgeries gave them a sense of power. In their "museum," on blue velvet they exhibited anonymous faucets and mannequins from a dump. Their museum was an orphanage for objects. There a faucet excavated from a dump was deemed as beautiful as a butterfly from a catalogue. The crippled objects didn't play supporting roles in this world anymore – they were the stars. Those objects were ritually purged from worthlessness and, by way of "declaration," made valuable. Due to their habit of scavenging dumps, this group of artists were accused of being "the necrophiliacs of a bourgeois world" by those rare critics who stooped to deal with them.

My father's friends had a weakness for deep conversations. They believed that the modern man was like Buridan's ass, equivocating between two symbols of his time. On his left side, there arose a diamond castle with checkered floors and crystal mirrors, filled with the sound of a clavichord. On the right side, there was a dump, a pile of junk and human bones as tall as a mountain. The castle and the dump were related, linked by an umbilical cord through Man. Valuable things were not just within the diamond walls. With Dionysius the Areopagite, my father's friends believed that God was able to manifest himself through the most disgusting things. The things dug up at the dump could turn into ornaments in the castle of civilization. "One should love damaged things as well," they said. "One should love something defective in order to find out the truth."

I admit that my impressions of my father and his friends are based on Olga's stories. In my non-expert opinion, my father's world contained something that always accompanies art and makes one heart-sick, something unpleasant, sinful, and feebly pretentious. I had a feeling that – as in the case of my grandpa, the Surrealist – there was an attempt to avoid the confrontation with the most ordinary problems of life by way of frantic inventiveness, the very problems that inevitably devour a man if he refuses to confront them. I may be malicious because I was never close to my father. The same gap existed between us as between Andrija and Grandpa Teofil. Forgetfulness covered my father's Belgrade from the fifties and the sixties the way lava covered Pompeii. One had to be an archeologist in order to reconstruct and consolidate the past so that the patches of the fragmented Belgrade life get sewn together. With inevitable malice I'm judging my father who rejected me. Be that as it may, I believe that in my father's time there was something that is implicit in the very word *art*, something unnatural and forged. Mystification was suffocating. There was something prone to ruin, something that makes us shiver, saddens us, prevents us from speaking – we can only wipe a tear from the corner of our eye... Something hydrocephalus, weak, betrayed, unable to cope with the world, lost in advance, hopeless.

And, of course, there was something glorious in my father's world.

CHAPTER 29

Last night, I winked at the Moon through the telescope.
She – not a thing. She just continued to amaze me
as she floated tragically in the void.
Leonid Šejka

The Moon.

The Moon is to blame because Olga fell in love with my father.

Belgrade is located in the backwaters of Europe which borders the Moon, and that's why the Moon has such a sovereign power over people and things in Belgrade.

The Moon is to blame.

The charming Irina wouldn't even have been born if Olga hadn't fallen in love with my father Andrija. An Italian proverb says that the Moon takes the woman to the man. The Moon is to blame. A walk in the moonlight in Kalemegdan Park brought Olga and Andrija together on a July night in 1960. On that night, from the walls of the Belgrade fortress one could see all the way to Pančevo. A sheet of moonlight covered the tops of trees and roofs. The moonlight was so strong it made the lawns and asphalt appear to be dusted with snow. Cats climbed the roofs to get closer to the Moon. In Belgrade, they turned off street lights because one could read in the moonlight. A retiree on a Kalemegdan bench spread *Politika* and grinned as he read the obituary of a contemporary whom he outlived.

Cicadas started to sing because the full Moon confused them. Olga and Andrija were sitting on "their" Kalemegdan bench. The Moon pulled them closer and called them... That night, the magnetism of the pox-faced planet was stronger than the Earth's gravity. Olga's skirt repeatedly rose above her head. The Moon swelled above the park that was neatly combed by the previous day's wind. Olga and Andrija held onto one another so that the Moon wouldn't lift them of the ground. They kissed and kissed and kissed...

Until the morning, Andrija and Olga walked the moonlit streets. They were completely alone in the dead-quiet city. Not even Adam and Eve could be more alone after they had been expelled from the Garden of Eden. The cicadas were singing in fake daylight after midnight. Andrija whistled softly. Olga shivered. Then a miracle happened: a stray dog attached himself to them and followed. All of a sudden, they looked like a family with a dog. Olga and Andrija walked side by side in the great wonder of that night. The Moon tirelessly spread white silk over Belgrade streets. Olga and Andrija never stopped kissing. And who was to blame? The Moon was to blame.

CHAPTER 30

A very sad letter to Irina

From the Dreamtime in which my father dwelled, I painfully landed back into my own time. As I was thinking about Andrija and Olga, I remembered my own love.

Oh, Irina. Do you remember?

I can't say that we had associated much before I ran into you on the Zemun promenade and then took you to the Sibinjanin Janko Tower. Four long years had passed since April 14, 1988, when we took a walk along the magnetic path by the sun-lit boats on the Danube. Something compelled us to touch each other with shoulders and elbows as we walked. And as we removed flying gossamer from our noses, you appeared to me in a light in which I had never seen you before. As if you tore off your mask just for me, emerged from the cocoon, and turned into a butterfly. The surprising Irina – that's the name I gave you that day. And you have never stopped surprising me since.

On my eighteenth birthday, you kissed me to make Boris jealous. For prom, you wore a dress the color of wine in which you looked voluptuous but well-proportioned, like female figures on Indian temples. From high school days, I remember you like a girl with commanding eyes who was hard to make laugh. The other Irina laughed as if she was freeing herself of something. I came to know the woman who made the best *quattro stagioni* pasta sauce in the world, who drove like a cab driver, who wore my sweaters and picked out my shoes and shirts. The laughing Irina was the girl I fell in love with.

During a few of our last conversations, I felt we didn't agree on anything. As if we had nothing to talk about any more. As if the butterfly that she turned into for my sake went back into its cocoon. I can't deny the change anymore. It is much easier for me to think that our time is crazy, but we aren't. We aren't, Irina. I shout this out with a question mark in my voice. And only silence comes back from your side. I don't think I'm expressing myself clearly because the things I'm talking about aren't lined up in my head very well.

What I'm talking about hurts. It hurts to talk about you flowering into a butterfly and wilting back into a cocoon. You probably were … you *are* … the love of my life.

Remember when we once talked about the most beautiful time of our lives at Zora's? I said that the most beautiful time of my life was a two-hour stroll in Korčula. I lied. The most beautiful time of my life was the walk we took at the Ušće. The most beautiful moment was when we came out of the Museum of Contemporary Art and Belgrade, at sunset, looked like a bas-relief in liquid bronze. I looked into your eyes – and fell in love as if I drowned.

"But fate has no desires," I can hear the hoarse voice of a folk singer on the radio.

Any love song I hear suffocates me.

Irina, everything is wrong between you and me.

CHAPTER 30
IN THE MIRROR

The monologue of the mirror spirit

My double is whining. He's whining because he's afraid his girlfriend might leave him. I would certainly leave him myself if that was possible. He's afraid of me, his double who lives in the mirror. He peers at me only superficially, trying to see only himself or parts of himself – the teeth he brushes, the hair he combs – but not me. When he was a kid, he tried to see me. He struggled to stay in front of the mirror as long as possible, gazing into my eyes. Then, all of a sudden, I looked frightening to him. To him I looked dead or crazy. He would scream and flee to his mom.

I have already introduced myself as the Covert Gentleman, Mr. Hyde. That's witty, I hope. However, that's not quite true. Mr. Hyde is the evil half of Dr. Jekyll. I'm not evil. I'm nothing. I'm everything. I'm the spirit of the mirror. I'm the spirit of the Millennium – the time of the changing of the masks. The young and the old, the rich and the poor, the happy and the sad bow to me.

For some reason, the author of these notes is hiding his name. He doesn't like to show his ID and claims that something gets twisted inside him each time a policeman asks him for identification. I'm not liable for his neuroses. I'll tell you – his name is Milan Đorđević. He's a historian and works at the Institute for Balkan Studies in Belgrade in the late 1990's. Milan Đorđević is upset by the fact that he can't be *all things* but only *one thing*. He's a butterfly on a pin, pinned down at a troubling moment in history. Milan Đorđević is sorry that he can't experience other forms of reality, that he can't see the world from every window and from every position.

I live in the mirror in his apartment. Even though I abide in the artificial space and timelessness of a Belgrade mirror, I'm connected to the spirits of the mirrors all over the world. I'm the mirror that mirrors the soul. I'll reveal a secret to you: the world has a common soul. Individuality is ... how should I say ... an imperative fiction. Every heart's beat pumps the soul of the universe through the world. I'm the poet of the Millennium. Everything I look upon – is mine. Everything I desire – is me. By way of empathy, I can turn into whatever I want. I'm the focal point of Ovid's *Metamorphoses*. Yes. I'm the Millennium. I'm as unnatural as Papageno and as natural as the rain. I'm poetry, I'm paradise. I'm the Expressionists' and the Romantics' union with Nature and the Soul of the Universe.

Ha! Ha!

Plotinus, Porphyrius, and Augustin interpreted the Delphi maxim "know thyself" as a path to knowing God in His countless forms. Milan Đorđević sees the whole world within himself because he sees the world through himself. He says that, to him, everything is a mirror – the eyes of a woman in the street, his tomcat, the book he reads, the letter he receives. He's trying to see his reflection in me, in his friends, in his city, in other cities, in everything that enters his field of vision. "Only a vampire can't see his own reflection," he says in desperation. I know that things are different. Like any other person, Milan would prefer to stick his head in the sand, in the garbage, or in the toilet bowl just to avoid facing me.

It's very hard to face the mirror.

Luigi Pirandello felt a deep aversion towards the *other* he saw in the glass plate coated with mercury oxide on the back. To Pirandello, his own reflection looked similar to someone's dog whose name could be … Flick! You know that dogs bark at mirrors. Do you know that cardinals in Alabama badly bloody themselves as they attack the sideview mirrors of pickup trucks?

At the beginning of the 19th century, a certain Mr. Cukić was in possession of the only mirror in the city of Kraljevo. The local constable came to Cukić's house. In the mirror's oval, he perceived a stocky bowlegged creature with an enormous moustache. The constable stepped back and pulled out his flintlock pistol. The pistol fired and the mirror shattered. When he realized what he had done, ashamed, the constable put the pistol back in his belt and said:

"I'm sorry, Sir, but nobody from around here has ever seen such a thing."

CHAPTER 31

On the fall of one of the Pillars of the World

This isn't a diary. This is a novel about the people who were Belgrade for me. This is a novel about the change that I feared because I couldn't see the end of it. The change I'm talking about didn't just affect the big world but also our smaller worlds – including ourselves. First of all, Bane wasn't with us anymore. Second of all, I began to wonder if Irina still loved me. Third of all, with some unease I noticed the contrast between Boris and Zora's previous and current relationship.

Previously, Boris would say that he loved Zora more than all of us together. When he went on a smuggling trip to Istanbul, he came back with a white kitten to keep Zora's cocker spaniel Mimi company. Zora named it Sun. The Angora kitten had two different eyes: one painfully blue and the other acid green. Sun rubbed against the whole world and against the air. It chewed on a thrown pencil and opened its lovely eyes wide as if it had just heard something amazing. Then it chased its own tail and hid from something nonexistent.

"Cats live in a fantasy world a lot," Zora explained.

In that way, Zora was very much like her kitten. To Boris, Irina, and me, she insisted that there were angels in Belgrade. She explained to us that those angels were like seagulls on the Sava: warm Mediterranean winds could caress them, but they chose to shiver in the cold eastern Belgrade wind because they were – special. Christ first appeared to Mary Magdalene because she needed him the most. The angels who live in Belgrade know that we need them more than anyone else in the world. If one could believe

Zora, these angels would, like projectionists, show a particular dream to each Belgrade sleeper every night.

While the angels showed their dreams to Belgrade sleepers, the military officers from Rebecca West's prophesies continued to play their million billiard games. In our city, thousands of people stood in line in front of foreign embassies waiting for their destiny.

"Imagine how cool it would be to have Giants' and Dwarfs' embassies in Belgrade," Zora said. "Then we could migrate to the land of dwarfs where elf small fry use flowers like trumpets."

The Russian author Aksakov said that he was – imagination. Zora could say the same for herself. She always lived in places she never lived in – in books and in dreams. Boris traveled a lot, but his trips didn't change him in the least. In contrast, Zora was a cosmopolitan who never traveled. She loved to talk about Pico della Mirandola and to imagine she lived in the blue Casa Batlló in Gaudi's Barcelona. In reality, Zora lived in an ordinary New Belgrade apartment in which a book case with art history publications took half of the living room. The apartment was on the top floor of a high rise across the street from Old Fountain. The Japanese Emperor's palace was traditionally called "a place above the clouds." That's what Zora called her apartment.

On a cloudy day, Zora was grey-eyed like the goddess of wisdom Athena. When the weather was sunny or when Zora was angry, her eyes resembled green-bottle flies. Those eyes noticed interesting little things. Zora noticed a passing truck full of wheat, covered with pigeons. She noticed that trees in bloom look like ghosts at night.

It was the spring of 1992. The countdown to the Millennium continued. After the wars in Slovenia and Croatia, the war in Bosnia made us sink even deeper into the ground. I couldn't keep quiet anymore, so I started publishing anti-war articles in independent newspapers. The protracted siege and murdering of

Sarajevo pained Zora even more than me. She felt shame for all the shameless. She started to feel like an accomplice in a crime just because she was buying bread and yogurt every day in the city in which she was born. Boris, however, had turned into quite a nationalist and started to fight with Zora which was something unthinkable before.

"You've changed," he reproached her.

"So have you," Zora retorted, stiffening with anger. "Nationalists like you constantly push us to go some place else. They don't have the right to do that to cosmopolitans."

Boris smiled and said:

"Compared to the Croats who are very much Croatian, the Muslims who are very much Muslim, the Albanians who are very much Albanian, you're not cosmopolitan but a fool."

"When I think about what's going on in Sarajevo, I feel ashamed that I'm alive," Zora retorted. "What do you want, us to pretend that nothing is going on, just like *ustaše* that slaughtered us in World War II?"

Boris shrugged his shoulders:

"So let's pretend."

Zora shook her head:

"Wrong. Wrong. So wrong… One can't turn one's eyes away, Boris, from those who dragged us into this horror."

"Listen," Boris said calmly. "I'm from here. This is mine. My country is my country – right or wrong. The Serbs didn't come up with that saying, the British did. Theodor Roosevelt was suspicious of people who loved other nations just like their own. Your problem is more than likely that you belong to the wrong nation." Boris smiled ironically. "You're an apple tree that would prefer to bear oranges. That's the definition of your cosmopolitanism."

"Boris, try to understand my position," Zora said in a serious voice.

"Zora, beware of your 'objectivity.' Your own folks won't love you if you don't praise them, and to those others you won't be any good even if you stood on your head. They have something against you from the start. An Armenian proverb says: 'Don't be a bridge – then people won't tread on you'."

"Boris, try to understand my position," Zora repeated.

"I can understand you but not those you advocate for," Boris answered. "Whoever understands their enemy's position for any other reason except to defeat them – is a fool."

And so, in Zora's apartment "above the clouds," the war introduced tension that had never existed between us before. I listened to Boris and, for the umptieth time, wondered if we actually know those whom we think we know. Pico della Mirandola was right to call man a miracle. I wanted to know if what Boris said about the war in Bosnia was also what he thought, or underneath those thoughts there were others, like underwear beneath clothes. Seemingly, there was a record which skipped in Boris' head, so he could hear only his own music.

"Please understand me," Zora pleaded to him for the third time.

"I'm not even trying to understand you," Boris shrugged. "Understand me if you want to."

Zora was shocked.

"So you're a fascist. I've never seen a fascist up close before."

"I'm not a fascist," Boris couldn't be calmer. "I'm an opportunist."

Zora stared at him with her grey eyes and asked:

"What's the difference?"

She finally enraged Boris with this remark.

"What are you doing here if you think that?" he readily countered. "Why don't you leave?"

Zora's eyes went green with fury.

"You want to drive me away?"

Boris lowered his voice.

"If you keep this up, you'll drive yourself away."

Zora was shaking. She glared at Boris with her stormy green eyes and ordered him:

"Get out of my house!"

Boris stood up slowly and said:

"Okay, but just remember that *you* drove me away."

With his gliding gait, the stocky young man left the apartment "above the clouds" for good. When he left, Zora's world shrank. I have already mentioned that our story is a story about the loss of support. It was not only the great pillar of the world which held the sky above us that fell. The small pillars that held our intimate worlds were also falling. For Zora, one such pillar was Boris. Zora was left behind in her room with me and her cat Sun and wondered what we were to do now. Should we lie down by the fallen pillar of the world and die like the tribesmen from Mircea Eliade's story? We had never been silent longer in our lives. Like dogs off their leashes, words ran away leaving everything nameless. All sounds went silent except for the hornet-like buzzing of the universe.

Zora got up and turned the TV on. On the screen, a goatee talked about the riches of the Templars. After him, Beki Bekić came on and sang showing a vast talent for jubilant laughter. Zora turned the TV off. Once again we sank into the horrid silence.

Finally, Zora said: "In every war, someone goes crazy. Zeus, please visit Boris. Christ, heal him so that he can see."

The way Zora frowned showed me that she was unable to express what she wanted to.

"I'm disappointed in the human race," she tried one more time. "I'd much prefer to be an animal."

I helplessly spread my arms and said:

"Animals also devour one another."

"Then a plant."

"There are poisonous plants."

"Then the air. Nitrogen," shouted Zora.

I looked out of the window and whispered:

"That's what we all have in store."

CHAPTER 32

Boris in the war

Soon after the beginning of the siege of Sarajevo, Boris put on a flack-jacket and went to Bosnia. I heard that, together with Dada and Double Hulk, he traded in gasoline, stolen computers, and cars. "He was my stand-in in fights as a kid," I tried to make excuses for Boris to Irina.

"To me, he's just an ordinary mobster," Irina argued. "It makes no difference whether he was your stand-in in fights or not. There's nothing romantic about the mafia. That's dangerous shit. That kills people."

When Boris returned from Bosnia, which was full of blood and smoke (the blood and smoke that had something to do with his presence there), he didn't want to see anyone, not even me, but he sent me a long letter that he wrote during the war. Boris was a very literate person. I don't know why that surprised me when I remember that, in middle school, he received a state award for his composition "Borders That Connect." I remember the times when that red-headed boy read two hundred pages every day.

"The important thing is to realize that there's no justice and no God; then you'll see how carefree one can be..." Boris wrote. "You wonder why I came here. Money is lying all around, one has to only reach down and pick it up. I don't want to live a hard life like my folks. I'll make my first million before I'm thirty, or I'll die."

I put the letter down and, in the oily voice of the actor Boro Stjepanović in the movie *Who's Singing Over There*, stated:

"Such a likable kid."

I picked the letter up again.

Boris wrote that he traded with the brothers Todor and Banjo Odić.

The face of skinny Todor Odić was stamped with frozen sorrow. Fat Banjo constantly sucked his teeth. "An unbearable man," Boris described him, "but a genius in trading in stolen and imported cars, and a great friend of mine." Boris and the Odić brothers loved to make their deals in the restaurant called *Picnic*. From a tree limb that was attached to the restaurant wall, a stuffed badger observed them. Above the badger, there were postcards of Leningrad and Sydney. The music blared. The singer rubbed her thighs and sang:

Others are to blame for everything
For my teary eyes, for your drunken lies
Others are to blame for everything…

A waitress approached the four young armed men sitting at the table and asked:

"What do you want, guys?"

All four raised their hands and said as one:

"Pussy!"

The painted beauty had an expression as if she was shooing away a fly and said:

"C'mon guys, be serious."

I put the letter down and laughed.

Boris wrote that the Odićes were blood brothers with some big shot from Pale.

Unlike Belgrade politicians who received envelopes stuffed with money from Dr. Kaligari himself, Boris had to earn his own money by sitting for days on end with the Odić brothers in the restaurant *Picnic*. The faded postcards of Leningrad and Sydney showed that, outside this room full of tobacco smoke, there was a world. Imagine that! Under the gaze of the stuffed badger, Boris made arrangements to sell cars with Banjo and Todor. Banjo Odić loved to put his finger in his ear and sing rustic songs. Boris thought: "I don't give a fuck. Just sing your songs, and I'll make some dough."

Todor Odić complained to Boris that two of his brothers were killed. Before the war, he was a Party secretary in the printmaking school in Sarajevo. Todor once told Boris:

"Had anyone said anything against Tito in front of me, I would've killed them. And now I would've killed myself for being such a fool. I didn't even know I was a Serb till the guys over there made it clear to me," Todor continued as he waived his hand towards the city. "Now I know what I am. In the hills around the city are the people like me – those who know what they are."

He wiped his moustache and added:

"You know when I'll start believing that the West is honestly dealing with us? When I see a Serbian kid crying on American television."

He had never read the American religious author Josiah Strong, but he held the same beliefs – the first city in the world was founded by the world's first murderer, so cities are the source of all evil. During the war, Todor Odić developed two passions: hatred against Sarajevo and love for religion. Despite his never ending sorrow and his appeals to God, Todor wasn't naïve at all. Once a Belgrade hoodlum tried to con him out of money. "What are you going to do now?" Banjo asked him out of concern. Todor made a sorrowful face, crossed himself, and said: "God willing..." The following week, the hoodlum's body was pulled out of the Drina.

Todor's son Novak was a sixteen-year-old curly-headed boy of exceptional beauty. Unlike his father whose expression was continually serious, Novak always had a grin pasted on his face. In his letter, Boris admitted that, despite himself, he suspected that the boy's good nature wasn't the only reason he smiled like that. Perhaps the source of the father's incurable sorrow could be found there. Todor pulled his son to his chest and put his moustache against the boy's cheek:

"Daddy's little hero! Will you fight the Muslim bastards?"

Novak straightened with pride.

Before the war, the boy's uncle, Banjo, owned a car junk-yard in Vogošća. His hands were so big that – whenever he wanted to open a pack of cigarettes – he gave it to Novak:

"Open this. It's too small for me."

Banjo had an SUV that looked like it was stolen from the UN and repainted. Novak asked his uncle to let him drive it.

"Don't fuck with me," Banjo responded.

For a moment, Novak's smile disappeared. Then his face lit up again and he asked Boris to let him drive his Jeep Cherokee. Boris turned to the constantly worried Todor.

"Should I let him?"

"Yeah."

"I'm also gonna ride along to see what kind of car you're driving," Banjo said.

In his letter, Boris wrote how Novak drove like he was flying. "Slow down, kid," mumbled Banjo from the passenger seat, while Boris, a bit tipsy, dozed in the back. "No problem, Uncle," Novak giggled. He turned off of the asphalt road and dusted the hedges along the dirt road. They passed a white flock of sheep. They bounced over a few bumps.

"What great shocks!" Banjo clicked his tongue in admiration.

Novak laughed and hit the gas. A bellow of white dust trailed after the car. Then something blew up and threw the car in the air.

"A mine!" Banjo screamed.

Boris held onto his seat while the car rolled over. At that moment, he swore to God that he would change his life. "If only I can survive this..." Boris murmured with his feet over his head in the overturned car. They pulled him from the car, his mouth full of broken glass. Banjo lost a leg, and Novak was buried.

All night, Todor was sitting by a cannon, drinking and firing into Sarajevo.

Boris was recovering from his contusions in Novak's room. He wrote to me how he stared at the image of St. Sava that stood on the night stand. That prince-turned-monk was the first to call the region where we live "the West's East and the East's West." Two centuries before Florentine Humanists, this educator held a vigil over Plato's dialogues. The blue eyes in the picture revealed a good man. However, Sava Nemanjić was too successful a diplomat for his kindness to account for all the aspects of his personality. If a single word could define who or what this thirteen-century Serbian saint was, it would be – diplomat. Boris sighed as he thought how the Serbs had apparently lost all talent for that kind of activity. St. Sava fondly repeated Pythagoras' words that the gods live between the worlds. One such fissure between different worlds was the Sarajevo gorge into which Todor, with teary eyes, fired his cannon all night long.

Boris wrote:

"I looked at the tear-brimmed eyes of St. Sava and I thought about the promise I gave on the day I almost died. So I told the saint: Forgive me. Who gives a damn about it now. It's wartime. Money's lying on the ground. I only need to reach down and pick it up. So what could St. Sava do to help me? In that room, to me he looked more like a hostage than a host."

When Boris got up the next day, Todor was still sitting by his cannon. He offered Boris a shot at the city. In the gorge, Boris saw the yellow building of the Central Post Office, the striped building of the National Library, the steeples, and the minarets. And he didn't rescind the offer. He wrote to me that at that moment, above the valley, in which the chimney smoke mixed with fog, he sensed the powerful presence of God. I trembled at the monstrous simplicity of that claim. I trembled even more at the thought that, most probably, Boris was completely sincere when he wrote that down. The Hindu god Shiva in his cosmic dance creates the world with the movement of one hand as he spins enormous energy into it. Meanwhile, he destroys it with the movement of the other hand thus releasing enormous energy. Boris felt enormous destructive energy in the destruction he caused himself. That's what he called God.

I put down his letter and whispered:

"That God of yours sure enough didn't appear to the mother who was trembling from the explosion in a Sarajevo basement."

That morning, by the cannon, Todor Odić told Boris that everything they agreed upon was still as agreed. Boris rubbed his hands. He did almost lose his life, but he also gained 200,000 Deutsche Marks in one fell swoop. And that was just a beginning of their partnership.

Todor promised he would pay for Boris' Jeep, and he put him in a van bound for Belgrade, together with a relative of his, an invalid. Forests and building flew by. The crutches were placed across the seat. Through his moustache turned green from tobacco, the invalid cursed under his breath. He cursed everything in the world, including his relatives Banjo and Todor. He split his curses impartially between the Bosnian Muslims, Croats, and Serbs.

"So many people got killed. So many got crippled," complained the invalid, drumming his fingers on the crutches. "My doctor told me to take a tranquilizer. So I take a handful each morning. That's what I do. With brandy. How are these guys going to build the future with invalids? With us? Buddy, there's no crutch for a crippled soul."

EPISTLE 32
IN THE MIRROR

In which I become a citizen of Sarajevo

Having read Boris' letter, I dreamed of Boris as a werewolf who stuck his ass out and combed it with a red comb.

Behind him, there was a landfill for piles of human hearts that people discarded because they didn't need them anymore. I don't know whether human beings are damned or blessed by their ability to consider more than just one point of view. People say that fools have it a lot easier, but I couldn't live like that. In my dream, I turned my back on Boris and – like I often do when I'm awake – I wasted my time standing in front of a mirror. I looked into my own eyes and instantly fell into the cosmos. I fell into the world beyond the looking glass and went through a metamorphosis.

I was still myself, but I wasn't in Belgrade anymore; instead, I was in the besieged Sarajevo.

For dinner, I ate snow with a spoon. My entire family was at the table. At first, the snow was white, but then it turned into the dirty city snow only to become bloody in the end. We were sitting beneath a bare electric bulb, scooping spoonfuls of the bloody snow from the plates.

People outside my dream and outside of the Sarajevo that was captured within my dream couldn't know how it feels when a hundred cannons fire. But we heard the rumble, and the sky shook. What about me, my mother, and my sister? Something within us died and we fell asleep with our hands on our knees, hiding in the bathroom while the shells rained on us.

"This is impossible," I whined. "They're crazy."

My heart skipped a beat when the glass shattered in the living room. I thought that it was the last whole piece of glass in the entire city. I looked through the broken window and saw that a high rise across the street was missing a whole story.

"They aren't in their right mind," I repeated.

A general with a smile of a tyrannosaurus and Dr. Kaligari's sleep-walking soldiers shelled me. Does no one really care? Not even you, God? Someone will stop it... Someone will raise a voice – I kept repeating a million times, until repetition robbed my words of all meaning.

In my dream, the whole planet was dark – except for one bright spot. It was my city, Sarajevo, burning. The city made of cotton, the city made of feathers. Prometheus suffered the ultimate sacrifice in order to give people fire, and then the same fire fell into Nero's hands. God was speaking from the flaming column, but I couldn't understand him. It appeared to me that the Creator was cynically indifferent towards human life.

I yearned to wake up, but there wasn't waking up from that dream. First the animals from the Pioneer Valley Zoo died and thus announced the death of the humans. The trees lining the streets, under which we used to kiss, were cut down for firewood. Stadiums and parks were turned into graveyards. That fall, my city became a frozen hell. The mouths of Sarajevo children chattered from cold. Adults' lips also shivered, but they didn't say anything. Before that, I was told that grown men don't cry; then I saw them crying. On the black market, cigarettes were more expensive than food. Those smoky pacifiers were the only thing that was left to the adult children who were abandoned by the entire world...

I stretched my arms to the sky.

The frightening silence between two detonations was the sole response.

I tore my hair out. I blamed Alija. I blamed the whole world. To no avail. The sorrow never left my soul, the spasm never relaxed. My city was burning. What was the reason for all of this? Attacks of rage alternated with attacks of fear. My life flickered like a lamp using its last drops of oil. The breath of death crawled underneath my shirt. The beating of my still living heart was the only thing that forced it out. I prayed to God to save me from a burial in a stadium or in a park. I prayed because I turned into a believer during the war. I wondered what kind of god the people who were shooting at us from the hills above, prayed to. I would never forgive them for forcing me to hate. But believe me I would've died of cold long before, had I not warmed myself with hatred. I poured a glass of homemade brandy, toasted to Allah above the Sarajevo sky, and whispered: "Deliver us! I know that the future will belong to those without bitterness, but... will I be one of those?"

CHAPTER 33

On tears and on the money that burns

The countdown to the Millennium was in progress. It was year 1993. In Belgrade, the rate of inflation was 306 million percent, and it was higher than the German inflation during the twenties. Heraclitus' invisible flames that lick the world made the money burn in our hands. In the course of a single day, the dinar lost its value a thousand-fold. I knew some people who didn't bother at all to collect their paychecks. As soon as she received her paycheck, Zora's mother would run to the Slavija square where unshaven men in short jackets whispered under their breath: "Foreign currency, foreign currency!" Zora's mother Mimica was able to buy three Deutsche Marks for her entire salary, while her good friend who graduated from college would get – seven marks. Sometimes she lent a little money to Mimica, so Mimica could buy five marks.

Zora told me how at one time Mimica's paycheck was overdue, and the traffic was jammed. Mimica was too late to exchange her dinars to foreign currency from the unshaven guys at the Slavija. At the time when Boris' friend Double Hulk let the engine of his Mercedes Benz idle for two full hours in front of a restaurant, ordinary people didn't have enough gasoline to drive to the hospital. For months, Zora's mother didn't drive her Yugo. As she waited for a bus in front of the Upin Store in New Belgrade for more than an hour, a sense of desperation overwhelmed her. She turned around and started to walk home. A truck passed her by and splashed her with gutter water. Mimica didn't stop. Drenched, she walked and shivered. The dinars she failed to exchange were losing value as she walked. When she got home, she sat on the floor and burst into tears. Ever since what the thinkers of the Enlightenment called "the accident of birth" had become so crucial in Yugoslavia, Mimica had been remembering that she was Croatian. She had spent her entire life in this fucking, beloved city of Belgrade. What should she do now? Where could she go now? She cried because of her city, because of her life, because she hadn't graduated from college, because of everything that had happened to us, because of her late husband and the lover who dumped her.

Zora came up to Mimica, put her hand on her shoulder, and lisped:

"Don't be afraid, Mother, we won't starve."

The mother simply waived her hand. In her overcoat, with her legs spread apart, she was sitting on the floor and crying the whole afternoon.

CHAPTER 34
IN THE MIRROR

**In which we continue to talk about the Millennium over
and over again**

1

Whatever is written in this book isn't particularly important.

Do you know what's important?

The coming of the Millennium is important.

In Moscow, the Tsar Cannon fired into the Tsar Bell. What was the reason for that?

The Millennium!

Learned men shake their heads and bray like donkeys. What's the reason for that?

The Millennium!

A fierce rhinoceros is running over the plain – an example of wasted energy. It resembles the people who start learning Sanskrit so they could read a two thousand year old prophesy regarding their destiny.

The Millennium!

On the Brooklynn Bridge, people hold burning sparklers in their mouths. They keep their eyes closed so they don't go blind.

The Millennium!

Pygmies climb on top of a baobab and, beneath the very clouds, pray that their destiny stays on the right course.

The Millennium!

The *Titanic* is emerging from the depths, lit up brighter than ever. The spectral band begins to play swing music like crazy.

The Millennium!

And what can we discern between the waves now? Aren't those the ziggurats of Atlantis? People with golden books containing all knowledge also emerge. So do the birds of Atlantis which became fish.

The Millennium!

The golden cities of Cibola and Norumbega brightly shine. Tigers with the brightest green eyes stretch out in them.

The Millenium!

Mozart composes an opera in honor of the arrival of the Martians. From the heart of darkness, there arises Gordias. This is going to be his last word before he, like a monk, takes a vow of silence that will last for a thousand years. He whispers:

The Millennium...

2

Some people visualize the Millennium as a spy who sneaks around corners. He will stealthily enter their lives and they will finally find him in bed sleeping with them. A screaming girl will jump out of her bed and dash into her parents' room:

"Someone's in my bed!"

The father will look aside to avoid seeing his daughter's nakedness and ask:

"Who's in your bed?"

The daughter will respond through tears:

"The Millennium!"

But, it will be already too late. By that time, the Millennium will be her legally wedded husband.

And not only hers. Everyone's. Both men and women will suddenly notice the Millennium's wedding ring on their finger.

CHAPTER 35

Which deals with my breakup with Irina

In the six years I spent with Irina, I often sat on the terrace of her house in Neimar and drank whiskey with Čedomir. In their living room, I would stop in front of the photograph of Irina's mother in a bikini when she was seven months pregnant. Irina loved to push her index finger against her mother's bulging stomach and say: "That's me." Because of that photograph, I came to love even Irina's mother, a woman with a hocus-pocus smile who praised the smart politics of Tarquin the Proud. Because I'm an idiot who's never gotten a driver's license, Irina took me everywhere in her Audi. I really liked the way she drove. My girlfriend was the most aggressive driver in Belgrade. I loved when we cooked together and selected wine from a wine shop. I even loved the traces of her lipstick on cigarette butts and cups. Irina wore my sweaters, so they smelled like her afterwards.

In springtime, Irina and I watched tree tops in bloom which – Zora was quite right there – looked like ghosts at night. In summertime, we lost our appetite because of the heat. In October, we kicked leaves in Kalemegdan and said: "Sooo much autumn." In wintertime, we had snowball fights, while snowflakes shimmered like silver underneath the candelabra of her house in Neimar.

Than came 1994.

The four hundred pound Mihajlo Ječmenica, better known as "the Dragon from Ub," achieved a great victory that year. In a competition in eating roasted veal, he defeated scores of people from Šabac, whose smallest representative was around two hundred pounds, while the biggest one was almost three hundred. The first church service in the Gipsy language was held in Serbia. The enormous rate of inflation was brought under control that year. And yet, in Belgrade, the most popular medications still were the tranquilizer *bensedin* and the ulcer drug *ranisan*.

I sometimes felt that the closeness between Irina and me was fading. Then I would convince myself that those were fantasies. We would succeed to manage the crisis and things would turn for the better. However, Irina really changed in 1994. Someone said that people can show tolerance only for what they aren't afraid of. Someone else said that one needs a minimal amount of security to be able to think in abstract terms. I was well aware that, in our circumstances, Irina didn't possess that amount of security. Yet I couldn't understand where that brutal, sudden change came from.

Over time, when I asked her something, Irina often failed to reply, wearing a thoughtful expression of a person who's peeing while swimming. It seemed she'd much rather spend an evening with her friends than with me. She dyed her brown hair red and became nostalgic about the time when she dated Boris. During a fierce fight, she told me that she felt fulfilled with Boris, while with me she felt empty. I still slept with Irina's body, but it was devoid of the soul that used to dwell there. Who took possession of your body, Irina? Who's living in it now? Did the devil, who's buying souls in bulk by way of TV, first buy Boris' soul and now yours as well? I prayed to God that yet another pillar that supported my world wouldn't crumble.

When Irina and I broke up, I felt dead inside all the time. I was facing the frightening unknown without any support except my own courage. I lived split between two opposite impulses: call her right away or never see her again. I didn't know what to do. I felt like biting my own shoe out of desperation or rolling in the street like a bird in the dust. I didn't know what to do. I didn't. I didn't. I didn't know what to do without her.

I tried to go cold turkey with Irina like she tried to go cold turkey with heroin. I kept saying: If I could live a week without her, everything will be alright. But first I had to live through the first day. I tried to avoid thinking that I *could* call her. Because if I thought I could call her, I would fall straight to hell. A storm would start in me. And everything that I am, my human pride and my convictions would turn into empty words. Oh, if only I could avoid thinking that I *could* call her, because...

Because Irina and I broke up in the real fuck-you-bitch-fuck--you-asshole Belgrade manner. In a way, our fight was worse than the fight that made Zora and Boris break all ties. There was nothing dignified in our breakup. As we walked from the railway station towards the *Hotel Moscow*, we went up Balkan Street, the street with the most hat shops in the world, and fought the whole time. We would've fought even more furiously if the street hadn't been so steep. And to be honest – it's hard to imagine that we could've fought more furiously. Maybe I should offer to my readers a nicer version of what happened, but it's boring to lie. We fought about how selfish I was and how she never listened to me anymore and then, all of a sudden – about Kosovo and the situation of the two million Albanians in it.

"They should all be fumigated," Irina said. "They should all be sprayed with insecticide like vermin."

"What!?"

"Pppssssttttttt!"

I threw my shoulders back, raised my head and told my love right in front of Janaćije Jonoski hat shop:

"Listen to me and listen good – go fuck yourself you motherfucking fascist!"

"Oh, no, no, you listen good," Irina squinted. "You're just a little pussy, a calculating, fake, *humanistic* pussy."

I couldn't believe what I heard. I hoped my love would shiver, get stiff, spew black foam from her mouth, and say: I'm not a vampire any more. But, to my horror, nothing happened. She continued to intensely stare at me:

"No, you listen!" I shouted. "You're a fascist – is that clear!"

"So say you, you impotent piece of shit!" she screamed and, with the tips of her fingers, slapped me on the face. It was a small but loud slap.

I slapped her back. A wisp of hair fell over her blood-shot eye, and she said:

"Get out of my sight, you little piece of shit. It's over. Get it? Don't you dare darken my door again, or I'll pay someone to break your legs!"

At that point she slapped me so hard I went deaf. My glasses flew across the street and left me nearly blind. I wanted to cut her head off, but I didn't. I restrained myself. Self-righteously offended, I turned around and went back towards the railway station. Everything in me buzzed and boiled with frustration. My legs trembled. I descended Balkan Street feeling *horribly* free. I was aware that no one would run after me. No one would shout the word I yearned to hear the most: "Wait!" I went away wearing a shirt Irina gave me as a gift and the shoes she picked out for me. But even if Irina had shouted, "Wait!" after everything that happened, I couldn't stop. So she would poison all those people? She would pay someone to break my legs? A decent person would never say things like that. One couldn't be like Bane's father – a jerk and a sane person at the same time – and still hope that, on average, they would turn out normal. One couldn't say things like that. I couldn't live with fascism. Or could I? After all, what did fascism mean? That was something unforgivable! But what did *unforgivable* mean?

I seethed inside. Yearnings and insults attacked me together, like the birds from Hitchcock's movie. Who were those Albanians to me anyway? Would they give up the best sex in their life for me? I knew that a breakup with a girl didn't look like a heroic deed from a novel, but the loss of Irina was a big sacrifice in my lonely life. I had spent six years with her. I believed that she had transformed me from an unpleasant eccentric into a bit less unpleasant eccentric. I wounded myself remembering the time we sat together, embraced, and listened to old songs. Tony Bennett sang for us: "Let me know what spring is like on Jupiter and Mars." Even the cheesiest love song hurt me. The word "banality" lost its meaning. The more trite a song was, the more it hurt. I would hear it and my throat would suddenly tighten. Oh, God! Oh, why? Why did that have to happen like that between her and me? I felt terribly insulted. Life itself insulted me. I felt like howling and howling from horror and jealousy like a brontosaurus on the verge of extinction.

I remembered that Boris once said:

"Irina, you're such a flaky tease. I wouldn't even bet five bucks that your future marriage would last."

It turned out Boris was absolutely correct.

Only he didn't know it would be his own marriage.

CHAPTER 36

The Marriage

Soon after my breakup with Irina, I learned that Boris and I switched places again. Every day, Boris took Irina out on the Sava in his large speed boat. They went on a vacation to Corsica. When they returned to Belgrade, they didn't eat at home but frequented restaurant-barges. Once they were quiet for a long time as they waited for their food on the *Amsterdam*. Irina gazed on the reflection of the sun on Boris' red mane. Boris stared at a seagull that hovered above the barge. He downed his whiskey to give himself courage, seized Irina by her hand, and said:

"Would you marry me?"

Instead of an answer, joy that resembled a quiet sob surged up from Irina's gut turning into a smile. Soon all their friends received invitations for the wedding. Irina used to daydream how she would marry on the beach in Bečići at the break of dawn with all her wedding guests barefooted. She got married in the church of Saint Salvation in Zemun at two o'clock in the afternoon, and all the wedding guest wore elegant suits – and shoes. Some of them wondered why the bride had such a mysterious smile while she circled the altar with the wedding crown on her head. The reason was because underneath her Italian wedding dress Irina wore no underwear. She and Boris managed to have a quickie five minutes before they entered the church where the priest declared them husband and wife. Such details always turned Irina on. As they left the church, Boris' best man Double Hulk threw coins to a crowd of Gipsy children. The wedding party posed for a photograph on the Zemun promenade by the Danube. The wind bore scattered confetti towards the river. Thinking it was funny, a Gipsy kid stood next to the newlyweds for the picture.

"I'll bite your head off," growled Double Hulk.

Boris intervened:

"Bro, don't – let him be."

The photograph documented the silvery glitter of the confetti around Boris and Irina's kiss. The Gipsy kid standing next to the newlyweds ducked his head between his shoulders and grinned like a little devil. In the background were the best man Double Hulk and his brother Dada. Dada who, in his time, used to don a flak jacket and fly to Zurich in order to rub out some of the "enemies of the state," was now Boris and Double Hulk's partner in foreign and domestic trade. I always felt uncomfortable in Dada's presence, and I always feared to look into his expressionless eyes. As for his brother Double Hulk, I liked him in my own way. On the Zemun promenade, Double Hulk paved Irina's path with one--hundred Deutsche Mark notes, so that she could step over that bridge of prosperity to the limousine. Then the party, honking their horns, drove off to the *Golden Coin Restaurant* in Upper Zemun. Irina's father Čedomir met them in front of the restaurant and presented a blue BMW to them as a wedding gift. Zora thought that all women with big bosoms were vulgar – except Irina. And she was right. In her wedding dress, Irina looked like she stepped from a poem. The waiters' jaws dropped as they stared at the most bosomy and the most elegant bride who ever set foot in their restaurant.

"What's up, buddy!" Čedomir shook the horrible Dada's hand. Boris winked in Čedomir's direction and repeated his favorite saying: "Once a cop – always a cop." My friends who told me about the wedding (as a true masochist, I wanted to hear every detail) couldn't even imagine that the two of them had known each other from before.

"You're a legend," Čedomir slapped Dada's broad back.

"No, you're a legend," Dada responded ceremoniously. Čedomir and Dada spent the entire party talking confidentially to each other. Čedomir's eyes were blue and teary, while Dada's were expressionless like coffee beans. Despite that, some thought they resembled each other like a father and a son. There wasn't any doubt that Čedomir and Dada shared a bond, unlike my father and me, or my father and my grandfather. Occasionally, one or the other would get up in order to slide a banknote in between the folds of a Gipsy's accordion's bellows. Only for them, with a smile of a womanizer, the singer sang "Verka" five times in a row.

Young men with crew cuts, looking like barrels squeezed into suits, danced at the wedding. Beauties in dresses the color of wine also danced. Grey-haired importers and fat-assed members of the cabinet danced as well. It was a good wedding and the question "What do you have to drink?" was met with the response "Everything!" Some of the guests got so drunk they forgot who married whom, in what city, and on what planet.

Nobody – neither I, nor Irina, not even Boris himself – knew that was not a wedding. It was vengence.

CHAPTER 37

On Boris Petrović's glory

1

Even though I tried to convince myself that I had put my breakup with Irina behind me, I must admit I barely survived the day of her wedding. Boris married her – I repeated before I went to bed. That's fine. Saint Paul said that it was better to get married than to burn. But jokes didn't help me. In my head, I started to repeatedly hear the lyrics of a song: "My unfaithful love married another guy, so I stayed unmarried, why oh why…" Just like me, you know that our subconscious isn't a DJ with particularly refined taste. But irony didn't help either. Irony never helps. I woke up in tears and said the only thing a man can say in such a situation:

"Farewell, my love."

It wasn't at all difficult to answer the question with which I tormented myself: "What did Irina see in Boris?" Boris and Double Hulk were doing really well. They traded in cars and gasoline at the time when the country was under international sanctions. They sold foreign currency at a higher rate of exchange and lent money at a high interest rate. They conducted some business in Prague. In Senjak, Boris built a house much bigger than the one his parents dreamed of their entire life. In that gorgeous house in Senjak, Irina and Boris lived for a year. I must say that Boris and Irina's wedding wasn't the most important event that year by a long shot.

On the historical scene, which assumed the form of the endless corn fields in Ohio, a peace accord was signed. If not peace of mind, the Dayton Peace Agreement brought to Bosnia at least the end of the bloodbath. In August 1995, hundreds of thousands of Serbian refugees from Croatia arrived in Serbia on tractors. Many Belgradians learned how to ignore the newcomers. The number of sold newspapers would go down whenever they featured a picture of the refugees. Once again, our Zora had a problem recognizing the country in which she lived. Once again she felt shame for all the shameless. Shame and despair were killing her. I was trying to "impartially analyze" the psychological blindness of the people around us.

"Our desires give the meaning to our words and take it away," I explained. "You can't tell people what they don't want to hear. Do you remember when Boris cussed out his mother who was standing next to him? She *didn't hear him* because that wasn't possible in her world."

That same year, in that same city, Irina and Boris lived happily. Or did it only look that way? Irina gave birth to a child. They named it Bojan. I heard that Bojan started to smile, first while sleeping and then while he was awake. All that time, I never saw him or his parents, but I knew that Boris started to suspect that Irina was fooling around with heroin again. He inspected her arms every day. It didn't work because she was shooting up under her tongue. Friends told me that they saw Irina bruised a few times. Who told me that? They started to fight more and more. Boris' prediction that Irina's marriage would not last turned out to be true. They divorced after a little less than a year. I believe Boris married Irina not for love but for revenge. He wanted to pay her back for the days when he rolled in the pigsty of fierce jealousy and randomly hit people passing by him in the Terazije square. He wanted to prove that he could live with and without her. I wondered if the final breakup with Irina hurt Boris as much as it had hurt me. Did he also whisper, "Farewell, my love"? Did his revenge bring him satisfaction? Was he as lonely as I was?

2

Boris continued to live alone in his house in Senjak. He called me, and I went to see him for the first time in three years. In a country in which retired teachers searched dumpsters for bread, Boris' house was a different world. The hardwood floor was made of five different types of wood. Boris was buying inlaid Baroque dressers. His dream used to be to make his first million before he was thirty. He certainly had much more now. When I entered, Boris was watching *Godfather 2* on his VCR. Hyman Roth was just telling Michael Corleone:

"We're bigger than United Steel."

My red-headed friend paused the tape and nodded. Then he got up and hugged me. Boris was alone in the house except for a skinny young man who looked more like a butler than a body-guard. I congratulated him on the birth of his child. I didn't say a word about Irina and Zora. Boris offered me a drink and told me what had happened with his parents. He shrugged his shoulders and murmured how his father had been an honest man his entire life. In a few words, he informed me that Auntie Maca had a stroke and vegetated in a state of early senility. He and horrible Dada went to see her the other day. Dada was sitting on her sick bed and observed her with his coffee bean eyes. His face was incapable of showing any kind of emotion. Boris held his mother by her hand. She didn't recognize him and kept saying:

"You're a good man."

The house in the village that Boris' parents spent their whole life building in order to earn the villagers' envy now stood empty. I said I was sorry. Boris waved his hand. He laughed and repeated how his business was doing well.

"Everyone has as many opportunities as his back can bear," Boris remarked with a stubborn smile. "I could also have waited for things to get better, but I know it will never happen."

I watched him as he smiled and wondered why he called me. He probably wanted me to envy him because of the house in Senjak the same way his parents wanted the villagers from Hicktown envy them because of their house there. Was he aware of that? I doubt it.

I was surprised that Boris' head and body had become somehow rectangular. Why is it that Belgrade businessmen become rectangular as soon as Fortune smiles on them? I didn't understand anything anymore about this man who was offering me a drink. The only thing I was still able to understand was Boris' sense of humor. His sense of humor hadn't changed at all. What had changed was his former cynical attitude towards every single ideology in the world. I remembered how both of us used to wonder how Irina's father Čedomir believed his own lies and identified his ideals with his personal gains.

"I don't understand how Čedomir is unaware of telling lies," I told Boris back then. "I always know when I'm lying."

"Good for you," the old Boris applauded me.

"I'd be insane otherwise, right?" I asked.

"You would be fake otherwise," he responded.

Now Boris was unaware of telling lies. The only difference between him and Čedomir was that Boris' materialistic ideology wasn't called communism but nationalism. Boris showed me an eighteenth-century icon from Cyprus he recently bought. Then he showed me a gold ingot that a certain Yuvachev sent him from a big gold mine in Tajikistan.

"Why don't you put a sniper on your roof to protect your icon and your gold?" I asked him.

Boris shook with laughter and said:

"No! I'll buy a white gorilla instead and keep it as a pet."

Boris poured us drinks and changed the tape in the VCR. He constantly refreshed our drinks as we watched the old movie about the fight between James Bond and Jaws.

"That's it. There goes our James," I shouted. "That's the end of him."

"He's sooo green," Boris responded. "They play with him like a cat plays with a mouse."

By three in the afternoon, we were both tipsy. Boris decided to take me down to the Sava. In his blue BMW we breezed by a bus stop crowded with people who just got off work.

"Look at the cattle jostling at the bus stop," Boris grinned. He rolled down the window and yelled with relish. "Fuck off!"

From the BMW we switched to Boris' speed boat. The warm wind licked our hair as we cruised from the Sava to the Danube. God, how beautiful that was! As we cruised in the speed boat, catkins floated above the rivers. The city glowed white above us. And life appeared to be really good. I jingled the ice cubes in my glass of Boris' whiskey as we hovered above the waters.

"This is the life!" Boris shouted.

I wasn't sure at all that what we had lived through in Belgrade the last ten years was the life. But I liked that the wind licked my hair in the speed boat at that moment. I was obviously sustaining the fragile illusion of normalcy as I lived in the state of deep denial. Just like my city, I gladly sank into oblivion. I was completely liberated from the idea that I was personally responsible for my own destiny. As I zipped above the water, I forgot that Tarquin the Proud ruled my country cancelling a smaller crime by committing a bigger one. I forgot that we spent ten years of our life in blood and humiliation. The country was in shambles, the prospects of the future ruined. But Boris and I flew above the water below the white city. We flew and flew...

As we flew above the water, Boris looked at me with the old sense of trust. My old friend smiled at me, and I responded to his smile, but it didn't mean the same anymore.

CHAPTER 38

"People are but floating shadows of soap bubbles that burst" – John Chrysostom

1

"Take a look," Zora pointed her finger at a cloud in the shape of a woman's profile. "That cloud looks like me."

We silently watched how the cloud with Zora's profile changed and dissolved in the sky. She gave me a rakish look and exclaimed:

"Interesting, huh?"

"What's interesting?" I asked.

Zora grabbed her shoulder and said:

"In my current human form, I feel responsible but I didn't feel that way when I was a river. There are truly times when I long for rest. I long to free myself from this body of mine, so I could run away following the rhythm of natural forces, flowing through the roots of plants, brooks, clouds, starry constellations, through all the forms of nature that Gaudi loved…"

In answer, I simply mussed up her bangs. We were sitting outside of a restaurant in Skadarlija. Dry linden tree blossoms were raining on our hair. Even though it was a peaceful afternoon, a band of street musicians played for some guests in the *Three Hats Restaurant*. The tall guitar player kept turning left and right as if scouting the scene. The violinist smiled like a rabbit. The big animal, the double bass, grunted in the background. The musicians sang:

Like a candle Jana burned,
Our love is stronger than consumption
I learned.

Zora winked at me and remarked:
"Interesting, huh?"
Stunned, I asked her:
"Did you hear what they're singing?"

Die, Jana,
I will die too,
In the afterlife our love will still be true.

That beautiful song about Jana was the most brazen hymn to death I have ever heard celebrating nothingness as the realization of true love. I first heard that song on that day in Skadarlija in the company of Zora Stefanović whom I used to call "my Platonic love" even in front of Irina. The dry linden tree blossoms rained on our hair. I often remembered the musicians' song later on, and it struck me as something stranger than the cloud with Zora's profile that we watched dissolve. And yet...

It was still too soon to fear.

2

Looking back, I can say that I was clueless as to what was going on. I didn't have a trace of suspicion. Zora's health actually did deteriorate, so we didn't see her as often as we used to, but we attributed that to her hypochondria. We called her on the phone and yelled:

"Come on, enough of that! Toughen up!"

Zora smiled tiredly. She constantly suffered from colds and flus, she felt weak, and her mother took her to doctors for tests. Again, we were clueless as to what was going on. Only Irina the witch once said without any compunction:

"Don't you think Zora might have cancer?"

That infuriated me so much I almost hit her:

"Shut up, you dumb ass motherfucker!" I cut her short. "How can you even mention something like that?"

I started to see Zora more often. I would place my hand on her head. I would caress her hair. I didn't like what she was telling me.

"Out of ten saplings they plant along a boulevard, one won't make it," she said. "It's the same with people. It'll be the same with me."

It frightened me and I pleaded with her:

"Don't be such a downer. You shouldn't think like that. Please."

The look Zora gave me was more distressed than the look Milan Ocokoljić once gave her. It was the look of a person who stepped into drying concrete and knew she couldn't get out. Life seen in pain is different from life seen without pain. One who's bedridden and the one who's sitting by the bed don't live in the same world despite the fact that they're holding hands. I was aware of that, but I tried to cheer Zora up and read funny articles from the *Evening News* to her.

I read to her about the farmer who entered his bedroom and saw some commotion under the blankets. He went out to the yard, returned with a tomato stake, and started to pound the blankets as hard as he could. Male and female screams resounded in unison, and then there was silence. Feeling good about his revenge, the farmer left the house and came across – his wife. "Good news," she said. "Your brother and his wife have come to visit from Germany. They're resting in our bedroom." The last sentence from the *Eve-*

ning News article read: "The brothers aren't on speaking terms anymore."

Zora rewarded me with a smile. Most of the time she didn't reveal she was aware of her serious condition. And yet, she told me once:

"When I'm gone, boys will still be making out with girls around the Pionir Basketball Stadium, trying to spread their thighs with their knees. The world won't put on a sad face because of me. Instead, it will stretch out like a lion."

A Chinese sage would say: life passes like smoke. Beyond is nothingness. A man shouldn't bind his heart to anything. Yet hearts are bound to things as imperfect as our city. Its multicolored lights kept licking its wet asphalt. The rain smelled like the sycamore trees along King Alexander's Boulevard. Belgrade breathed in sync with its urban pulse. The city didn't have any time for us. It was indifferent to the people who – like aphids – glided along its surface. Belgrade didn't care about Zora Stefanović who was saying goodbye to it with her last glance.

I didn't know how long Auntie Mimica changed labels on prescription bottles so that Zora couldn't see what she was taking. She took her to the basement chambers in the Central Military Hospital probably for radiation treatment. They slid her inside some dark underground cylinders and closed the lid after her. I felt my throat tightening as I thought about everything such a good person had to go through. Zora would grab her mother's hand:

"Help me, Mom. Don't let them put me in those things."

"You have to, sweetie!" her mother responded.

Auntie Mimica tried to boost her daughter's spirit all the time. Late at night, she wept alone in the bathroom. Auntie Mimica was not the only one doing that. During the last decade of the Millennium, many people were weeping in Belgrade.

Zora grew weaker and weaker. She quit going outside. During her illness, Boris never visited her. Irina did. Bane was in America. I tried to visit her as often as I could. By that time, I figured out what was going on. When I figured that out, I repressed an impulse to scream and continued to act normal. I would come to read to Zora, and Auntie Mimica watched me with gratitude. I tried to cheer up "my Platonic love" with my babbling. It seemed to me that, if I fell silent, death would immediately rush into the room. I read to Zora how the situation in Bosnia was calming down. She gave me a tired smile, pointed at her stomach, and said:

"Bosnia is inside me."

Since the very beginning of the siege of Sarajevo, Zora felt like an accomplice in crime simply because she continued to buy bread and yogurt every day in the city where she was born. On one hand, I loved Zora's moral awareness. On the other hand, I hated the theory which lumped together all hemophiliacs, lesbians, crossed-eyed children, dandies, criminals, and PhD's and found them guilty – until the opposite was proven. Zora believed that the tragedy that befell us all was much greater than people dared to believe. She suspected that the lives of people over thirty in our country were ruined. As for the others – it remained to be seen. She insisted that women were braver than men. In front of the parliament building, she held candle vigils in support of Sarajevo and didn't hesitate to say things "one wouldn't dare say."

"I don't give a flying fuck about their taboos," she used to say. "Intellectual cowardice inevitably breeds stupidity. Despite their macho attitudes, fools are castrated. I'm sick and tired of those who have the courage to kill but don't have the courage to think. I'm sick and tired of sneering cowards afraid to express what they think. I'm sick and tired of jerks whose only identity is derision."

All of a sudden, in December of 1996 there was more light inside the people of Belgrade than before. The three-month long demonstrations against Tarquin the Proud began. On Belgrade streets, students waved the flags of all countries. Female students bared their breasts to the black line of ogre-like riot policemen. It was a political climate change that Belgradians called a miracle. In the streets, complete strangers treated each other with ultimate civility and kindness.

The official news programs denied that anything extraordinary went on in Belgrade. People connected tubas to vacuum cleaners, beat on cooking pots, and – during the time of the evening TV news – made all kinds of noise any way they could in order to drown out the official lies. That was the first rebellion against the glowing, lying screens in the world. From New York, Bane wrote to me that it seemed American journalists didn't like the possibility of a popular rebellion against TV. The three-month long daily demonstrations in bitter cold left me with a sinus infection, while the situation in Belgrade ingloriously calmed down by the end of the winter. And yet, in the course of those three months we felt the same life-giving surge of enthusiasm that made the statues startle again like they did during the Belgrade New Wave Period.

It was too late for our Zora. Accumulated frustration was killing her slowly. Shame and hopelessness had been suffocating her for too long. In his diaries, Kafka described the telegraph-like communication between the brain and the other organs. The brain wired: I can't bear this anymore. Can someone shoulder the burden that's crushing me? Whenever an other organ takes on the burden that's oppressing the psyche, we fall seriously ill. That's what happened to Zora. The members of the tribe that Mircea Eliade described would lie down and die when the totem pole that supported their world collapsed. The pillars that supported our world had been falling like dominoes over the course of the last six years.

3

Zora Stefanović smiled for the last time when she was in the hospital, while her mother was reading the 23rd Psalm to her:

"The Lord is my shepherd; I shall not want. He maketh me to lie down in green pastures: he leadeth me beside the still waters…"

Auntie Mimica took a deep breath to stifle a sob. She tried not to swallow words as she was reading. Tears slid down her neck as she continued:

"Yea, though I walk through the valley of the shadow of death, I will fear no evil: for thou art with me; thy rod and thy staff they comfort me…"

Zora wanted to be buried in their family crypt in Herceg Novi, so she could "watch the sea" even though she was dead. Her mother promised her that, but she buried her in the Central Cemetery, so she could visit her. Zora's tragic Mediterranean face in the coffin looked more chiseled than ever. I approached her and told her in complete sincerity:

"You were the best person of all of us."

Shovelfuls of earth fell on the coffin. With the nails of one hand I clawed the palm of the other. I couldn't see anything for the tears. The cemetery looked endless and hopeless. Only Auntie Mimica, Zora's sister, Irina, and I were in attendance. Later on, a few more people from the School of Applied Art also came. Boris didn't show.

"What do I live for now," Auntie Mimica asked.

By the mound, I asked myself if Zora had ever had a boyfriend. Did she ever kiss?

She was an odd cosmopolitan who – before this last journey – had never traveled anywhere.

She wanted to visit the Grand Canyon which she imagined was like an enormous park designed by Gaudi that took two billion years to complete.

She was positive there were angels in Belgrade because we needed angels the most.

The shovelfuls of earth landed on her coffin and resounded and resounded and resounded...

I was supposed to call Bane in America later and tell him about Zora's death.

"What are you telling me, Milan?" Bane began to cry.

"I'm telling you," I answered, shocked by the small spasm of delight in my chest, "that our good Zora was buried yesterday."

CHAPTER 39

In which Bane Janović and his invisible companion are awed by the "enormous subtlety" of the Grand Canyon

Dear Milan – Bane wrote to me – do you remember how many times we wondered if Zora had ever had a boyfriend? The answer is: She did! It's the time for me to tell you that she wasn't just my friend. She was my love.

May you never experience the state of mind I was in after I had returned from the Slavonija battlefield. After the war, I tried in vain to overcome my disrespect for life. Sorrow is too weak a word to describe what I was feeling twenty-four hours a day. In the midst of Belgrade's bustle, I hummed Morrison's song: "People are strange when you're a stranger, faces are ugly when you're alone..." I would see only Zora. Every evening we went out for a walk. Even though we walked side by side along the same streets, she was in the ordinary world while I was in hell. Zora bridged the gap between the worlds, and she was the first to touch me. That was different from how other women touch you. She was not a woman – she was a wonder and her touch felt so... deep. When we separated after the first kiss, buildings swirled around us. The sky was a starry maelstrom above Belgrade. I stammered:

"Now I don't know which street we're on."

Zora said:

"I don't know what city we're in."

Once, stupidly joking, we promised each other that, whoever dies first will let the other one know. Different continents aren't an obstacle for the soul. I believe the dead Zora is now with me like she wanted to be when she was alive. That's why I decided to take her to the Grand Canyon that she always dreamed about, so she can see it through my eyes. Our trip didn't cost very much because the dead don't pay for tickets. That I couldn't see Zora didn't mean she wasn't there, huddled on a plane or car seat next to me. During our entire trip, I held my invisible companion's hand and pointed out every interesting detail of the New World:

"Look, Zora, look!"

I have a relative in Las Vegas, so I first showed the different styles of that city to the invisible art historian, Zora Stefanović. In the course of six days, we got tired of the cascades of light on buildings, the moving elevators, and the laser shows. At dawn on the seventh day, we left Las Vegas, the city located in between the Mount of Dawn and the Mount of Dusk, and went to see what we actually came for – the Grand Canyon.

The daybreak displayed such a sky that I felt all azure inside. The mountains of Nevada looked like gold glaciers. The heat became oppressive at the moment when Lake Mead shimmered in front of us. After the Hoover Dam, there followed the devilish architectures of Arizona. Then vast spaces opened. So blue! So vast! Human vision was limited to a narrow frame within that endless vista. I whispered to my invisible companion: "Look, Zora! Look!"

We drove on and on. The Arizona landscape increasingly turned into prairie and brush-land. It was fit for cattle grazing. The onslought of beauty against the car windows ebbed. There was nothing else to show Zora, and my tired eyes were closing. Suddenly, a summer miracle happened! The sky became angry. Raindrops slashed across the windshield. Click-clack! The wipers came on. The wheels of the car in front of us spewed rain-dust. The windshield went blind with water. The wipers didn't help much. "We're going to die," I told my relative who was driving. "We're going to die!" We emerged from the wall of rain as abruptly as we entered it. The ground was dry. It didn't rain here at all.

We sped up along the dry highway. Then we noticed that a policeman locked on us. We slowed down, and our car emitted a halo of light. In the midst of that vast space, we turned into angels. We coasted at a very slow pace until the policeman drove away. With our halo still on, we glided into the Grand Canyon National Park. The Indian woman at the gate flashed her turquoise earrings and said:

"Today the park is free."

A grove of stunted trees offered a poor introduction to the magnificent sight we expected to see. Nothing hinted at the proximity of the Grand Canyon except maybe for some blue mist between the pines. I became increasingly impatient. And then – to borrow the words from Borges' story "Aleph" – *I saw it*! I drew a deep breath, thrust my chest out, and focused my eyes. All of a sudden – I was in the sky. As I stood on the ground, I had an aerial view. The entire vista became an enormous embrace. My God! My God! I just looked. I was just silent –and grateful, grateful…

Before that sight the soul shrank and shivered, and then the body shivered. "Those are temples," it occurred to me as I observed the gilded peaks which towered over the canyon. I thought of God. I thought of Zora who always recommended to me to see this place.

"Wow, how awesome!" I smiled a tiny smile. "Zora, here's your gigantic Gaudi park that took two billion years to complete! Look how magnificent it is. Look!"

I laughed out loud and sighed. The soul, spun into a wick, pulsated in the place where my ribs joined. My eyes took in an enormity of blue air. Colors too. And – it was vast! Vast! I looked and absorbed like a sponge for beauty. I couldn't find words. I found humbleness and awe. *Vast subtlety* – those were the words. With a motion of my arm, I pointed out the vast subtlety to Zora.

"It's eighteen miles wide," my mustached relative noted, "and it's deeper than the Himalayas are high."

I believe that I observed the Grand Canyon through the eyes of an art historian. I lent my eyes to Zora and she, in turn, lent me her sense of color. The pinkish-purplish colors warmed the endless space of the canyon while the bluish-grayish ones cooled it. Like bridges, azure strips hovered in the air. The sunset gilded the faraway rim of the canyon. The paths down which people on mules descended into the canyon glowed white below me. The rock on the right looked like a gigantic chunk of gorgonzola. On the left, the rocks had the color of cinnamon and the color of clouds. An angel put a drop of milk into that palette, so it was hard to describe it. All shades were filtered through the bright prism of the canyon's endlessness. The most beautiful color was the bright color of vastness.

A new light shone and the landscape changed. The entire scene looked like it was powdered with chalk dust. That was the color of the soul. That was the color of the Belgrade walls from the dreams.

"Look, Zora! Look!"

My down-to-earth, kind relative noted that my mood was too "solemn" and, in his good-natured way, tried to bring me back from that state. He wondered out loud if we had parked our car in the right place. As for me, the car might as well have disappeared. With his finger, my relative pointed out some squirrels to me. The squirrels, which I otherwise like, might as well have disappeared too. My relative talked about some evergreen berries that smell nice. But I went through a religious experience and didn't want to profane it with babbling. If I could just look without talking! Maybe my soul was trying to assume the vastness of what I saw. For a short moment, maybe I tried to reflect the sky in a thimble of water.

"People view the Grand Canyon from helicopters and planes," my relative explained. "It's now forbidden to go beneath the rim."

I tried not to offend the kind man who did me a favor and brought me here. I responded politely, ripping a chunk of my flesh with each answer. I only wanted to be quiet. I only wanted to drink the colors of the Grand Canyon with my eyes.

In the incomprehensible layers, I observed the metamorphoses of stone which morphed like clouds.

"Look at those separated rocks on the left that look like swirls of whipped cream on a cake!" my relative exclaimed. "In a year, they'll collapse."

The enormity of time matched the enormity of space. "You've never taken in that much time in a glance," asserted a billboard. To tell the truth, I was really amazed by the span of time I faced. Today, all mankind is fascinated by an anniversary as trivial as the end of the second millennium of the Christian Era. The gorges and heights around me were two million millenniums old. Which means that the Grand Canyon was twenty thousand times older than the members of the *homo sapiens* species who snapped their cameras at it.

Tourists, the simian ants, crawled about the canyon and talked nonsense in all the languages of the world. They wouldn't chatter like that in a cathedral. Or would they? If I could only yell: "Shut up!" so that they would all turn into stone sculpture for three hours and let Zora and me observe the bluish and golden cliffs in peace. I watched the miracle that quiets the soul and thought: "It's impossible to tell a lie in this place."

At that moment, the sky became smoky. A cloud darkened the Isis Temple. Cold rain dampened us even though a section of the sky remained blue. A squirrel hunched on a wall. We ran to seek shelter from the shower. There was a wooden castle and a beautiful village with stables from which the mules departed. We found cover in a glass pavilion for selling souvenirs. Through the glass, we again saw that the canyon was endless. Usually, beauty comes in small packages. But this before us was as beautiful as it was vast. Me and my invisible Zora smiled a tiny smile before the vast subtlety of the sight.

While Zora and I smiled, the rain stopped again. As soon as the sky cleared, we spotted a purple mountain touched with the most delicate shade of gray. What looked like a huge pearl was the focal point of the canyon – the Isis Temple. I realized that the Grand Canyon wasn't a park – it was the temple of the world… The peaks bore names of all gods. The peaks were temples indeed. In the Shrine of the Whole World I prayed for the soul of her who, invisible, accompanied me on this journey. As I prayed for the girl who believed that there were angels in her city, they were around me:

Diana's Temple, Scorpion's Ridge, Grandview Point, Confucius' Temple, the Tower of Ra, Osiris' Temple, the temples of Horus and Shiva, the Tower of Seth, the temples of Isis and Buddha, Hopi and Mohave Points, Cheops' Pyramid, Deva Temple, the temples of Brahma and Zoroaster, Wotan's Throne…

And finally – the Bright Angel's Point.

Tears blurred my view of that peak and I whispered to the invisible Zora:

"This point is yours."

CHAPTER 40

The ambush

Everything would've been fine if the younger Vukotić hadn't married the daughter of a certain Sinister Dude. During the wedding reception, the Sinister Dude invited his son-in-law to have a smoke with him. In the courtyard, he put his hand on Vukotić's shoulder and asked him if he needed anything. The younger Vukotić had not forgotten the man who had crippled his brother with a spear-gun. For years, he wanted to get even with Double Hulk as he remembered his own cowardice and his betrayal of his own brother. So he asked for Double Hulk's head.

"What you're asking for is no small matter," the Sinister Dude drawled.

"I'm asking a great man a great favor," the sweet-tongued Vukotić responded.

Vukotić was very much aware that what he was asking for wasn't a small matter. First, Double Hulk had a Mercedes Benz with bullet-proof glass, so no one could stage a classic Belgrade hit and take him out when he entered his car. Second, killing Double Hulk meant starting a war with Boris Petrović and the horrible Dada. But, it was the right time for generosity. When can one relax if not at a wedding, the Sinister Dude thought. He nodded and gave Double Hulk's head to Vukotić as a wedding gift.

Unaware of this fateful exchange, Boris Petrović and Double Hulk went to Borča on Sunday, May 20, 1997, to attend a dog fight. The whole neighborhood smelled like dogs. The owners proudly walked their rottweilers and schnauzers. Some angry jerk hit a bull terrier on the head so hard that everyone turned around at the sound.

"What's that scar on your ear?" Boris asked Double Hulk as they walked.

"It's not easy being a chivalrous knight, brother!" Double Hulk frowned as he patted his German shepherd. "You remember Zita?"

"She used to be one hell of a woman," Boris responded.

"Sure thing," Double Hulk agreed. "She's nuts, you know. Two days ago I went to the Gipsy quarter right behind my house and there I spotted Zita and one Nina the whore. Both pregnant to their gills by the same guy, some Miki the dealer. Imagine that, two pregnant chicks going at each other with knives. I rushed between them, and Zita cut me across the ear. I bled like a pig."

"Over your new Ellesse sweats," laughed Boris.

"I smacked her face and pull out a gun. Throw those knives down! On your knees, I shouted."

"So they knelt," Boris smiled a little smile.

"Both of them knelt. Both pregnant. I shoved the barrel of my gun in Zita's mouth and then in Nina's. What now, you stupid whores? You want to suck my dick? C'mon, on your feet. I kicked one in the ass, then the other. I threw their knives down a john and went back home to wash myself."

Boris laughed.

Double Hulk shrugged:

"It's not easy being a chivalrous knight, brother!"

At that moment, Pera Panajotović, *aka* Jungle Jim, approached Double Hulk and notified him that it was time for his Rex to fight. The bet for the fight was a thousand Deutsche Marks. The German shepherd Rex was supposed to engage the boxer Aga who belonged to some hick from Češljeva Bara near Golubac. They said that the hick viciously beat his dog every day in order to make it even meaner. Double Hulk squeezed Rex's ears between his palms, kissed him on the back of the head, and let him go. The shepherd with the almond eyes and the boxer with a crumpled muzzle charged each other and started to wrestle in the dust. In no time the dogs turned into a growling whirlpool of bloody fur. The fans growled more fiercely than the dogs. Among the voices of the cheering ruffians, there rose Double Hulk's roar:

"Rip its throat out, Rex!"

"Get 'im, Aga!" the hick from Češljeva Bara yelled.

The ugly boxer managed to lock its jaw on the shepherd's leg. The dog whirlpool grew bloodier. Then blood began to spew. Everyone groaned when the boxer bit off the shepherd's leg.

"Break it up!" Pera Panajotović shouted.

Double Hulk ran into the ring with his gun drawn. He kissed the crippled Rex and shot him in the forehead. He paid Pera Panajotović to take Rex's body back to his yard where he wanted to bury him. The boxer's owner didn't even think about asking for the money. When Double Hulk remembered to look him up, the man had already disappeared.

As they crossed the Danube back towards *Hotel Yugoslavia*, Double Hulk's eyes were full of tears.

"It's not fit to say, but a man can come to love a dog," he said with a lump in his throat.

"Yes, a man can come to love a dog," Boris agreed.

"It's not fit to say," Double Hulk continued in a hoarse voice, "but killing Rex was more painful to me than burying my father."

They drove away in Double Hulk's Mercedes Benz towards the old Merkator Shopping Center. There they were supposed to meet with a certain Nikšić who had just arrived from Prague. The two friends left the car in order to stretch a little in the May sun. Double Hulk took out the last cigarette and crumpled the empty box. Boris called Nikšić who had failed to show up. Double Hulk ground the cigarette butt with his foot and asked for another cigarette. Boris took out a pack from his pocket and dropped it. As he bent down to pick it up, he saw a BMW approaching them, the same as his except for its metallic color. One of its windows was sliding down. The whole street started to dance to the chatter of a *Heckler and Koch* sub-machine gun. Kiosks, passers-by, and green buses started to dance. The reflection of the sun on the windows of the surrounding apartment blocks also began to dance to the chatter of the sub-machine gun. The burst caught Double Hulk across the chest. Boris got hit in the thigh. He drew out his gun and fired. The BMW's tires squealed as the car zig-zagged. Boris fired again and shattered the back windshield of the receding car. When the BMW disappeared from view, Boris dragged himself to his friend who was gasping. Double Hulk raised his head which resembled the bearded heads in Assyrian bas-reliefs.

"Are you dead?" Boris shook him.

"No. I'm alive."

With those words, Double Hulk spewed out a mouthful of blood.

CHAPTER 41

The funeral

After Double Hulk's death, two whole pages of obituaries appeared in *Politika*. In one of them Double Hulk's picture looked like a mug shot. Underneath it, the caption read: "Your dear face and kindness will be eternally cherished in our hearts. Your Neki and Shark."

At the funeral there were a number of guys with gold chains that wouldn't put even Montezuma to shame. The guys approached the open casket and nodded at the deceased. Someone whispered that a pound of gold in a shape of a chain vanished somewhere between the crime scene, the morgue, and the chapel. The guys who had danced at Boris' wedding party waited in line to express their condolences.

Double Hulk's parents were dead. His aunt, who was sedated, accepted the condolences. They said that the aunt muttered the whole time: "Nešo, my boy, let this be a warning to you." Her eyes were joyful when I squeezed her hand. I cast a fearful glance at the open casket. The mannequin in it obviously wasn't Double Hulk. I couldn't wait to get out of that chamber and its scent of death. As I left the chapel, the sun blinded me. I rubbed my eyes and saw the priest and some well-dressed girls arranging the pageant of wreaths.

When the funeral pageant moved, a woman behind me started to cry. When the music started to play the death march, the woman began to wail.

"Are you crying because of Nebojša or because of the music?" her son asked as they carried a wreath.

I carried a wreath with some buzz-cut little bull.

"Brother, what can I say," the little bull sighed. "They killed our Nebojša."

Never in my life had I called Double Hulk Nebojša. Had I died a day before, I wouldn't have known his real name. I watched girls with heavy make-up who looked really good in black. I watched the short necks of the guys in front of me. The funeral pageant moved along at a terribly slow pace. My shameless mind remembered a commercial ditty for some funeral home from Požega:

A living soul couldn't breathe within
A Radiša Đurđević coffin!
The master's hand made everything air-tight
So the dead man may rot in peace alright!

I suppressed a smile and looked over the gloomy pageant. Boris and Dada were nowhere to be seen. The little bull who carried a wreath with me noticed my glance. He was the nephew of Boris' mother, so he used to see the two of us together when he was still a boy. Out of the side of his mouth he confided in me that, the day before, the horrible Dada threw a hand grenade into the room where Vukotić and his pregnant wife were eating lunch. Last night, he and Boris fled to Thessaloniki to wait for the situation to calm down.

Slowly putting one foot in front of the other and carrying the wreaths we finally reached the grave site. On the wooden board it read: Nebojša Dokmanović. His aunt from Belgrade, with her tranquilizers, stood by the grave with some Montenegrin woman with deep-set eyes. It would have never occurred to me that Double Hulk was a Montenegrin. One doesn't really consider the origin of someone so urban. The paid mourners started to wail. Within rural culture, wolfish howling of paid mourners are seen as an expression of true sorrow. The ritual act has an advantage over sincerity. I shuddered. I wanted to flee from those metallic voices that froze the spark of life in a plant, an animal, and a human being. I shielded myself with the commercial ditty of the funeral home's owner from Požega:

Our products are first-rate, our customers rave,
No way your dead can escape the grave.

Then the uncle from Montenegro rose up by the grave. With his teary eyes, he looked straight into the myth. Then he lifted his hand to silence the women and began a dirge:

"My falcon, my Nešo! There's only one thing I can't forgive you... Why did you do me this injustice and went to the grave before me? Why didn't you wait for your time? Why did you leave me behind in misery?"

The uncle turned his epic nose towards the aunt who had already been on medications for three days. He looked her in her joyful eyes. Suddenly sobered, he said in a completely normal voice:

"You really didn't have to use this ugly picture of him, did you?"

Then, with a characteristic ease, he switched from the normal mode back to the epic mode. He lifted his hand one more time and wailed:

"Why did you wrong me so..."

This ability to switch modes, to enter and leave the epic at will, stunned me. So I thought: "This faked trance holds the answer to everything that has been happening to us in the last eight years." The uncle addressed the dead Double Hulk as if his nephew was blind but not deaf. As if at an auction, he pointed out to the deceased those who had come to see him off.

"Your friends from the Judo Association have come, Nešo. They want to salute you one last time!"

The guys with gold chains had faces of stone, like soldiers. The crippled aunt from the boonies wailed loudly. A few martial artists cried like the rain. Two of them delivered speeches. Two heavily painted women in black first looked at each other with animosity over the wreaths and then supported each other. The first clots of earth thudded against the coffin.

A woman behind us started and exclaimed:

"The deceased has it the worst!"

We all threw a handful of dirt on the coffin. The gravediggers quickly filled the grave. A whole mountain of wreaths rose above the mound. I wondered if the urchins would collect the flowers from Double Hulk's funeral and take it to the florist to resell.

The aunts discussed the type of marble for the headstone. There was no one to take my leave from. I waived to the guy who carried the wreath with me and slowly snuck away from the funeral party. I walked past the picturesque graves at the Central Cemetery. I went by the bronze monument of a guy whose relatives stuck a sports newspaper under its arm every day. From a black marble headstone, the members of a family watched me while smugly leaning against the Mercedes Benz in which they got killed. I passed by the monument of a boy who was sitting in a bronze toy car. Kitsch is a historian's friend, I thought. Kitsch tells us more about people than good taste ever can.

Following the paths that grew quieter and quieter, I went to a distant lane. I stopped in front of a gray marble headstone. I looked at Zora's picture and started to cry. I didn't grieve after my Zora through ritual wails of mourning women but through hot, silent tears. Then I noticed that someone was standing next to me… Irina was the last person I wanted to let see me crying. And yet, I didn't restrain myself. I let my tears run.

Irina's eyes screamed. She was now a divorced, lonely woman who wasn't young anymore, maybe on heroin again. It occurred to me that all these years she'd been sweeping dirt under the carpet, so now she seemed to stand on a heap of garbage rather than on Zora's mound. With her screaming eyes, she looked at me from that heap.

"Milan," she spoke in the voice of a blind woman who recognized a familiar face beneath her palms. "Milan…"

She made a swinging gesture with a bouquet of flowers she was holding. With that gesture she encompassed the entire cemetery.

"The times we live in have killed love in people," she groaned. "And we live on love. Whatever we do, we do on love."

She horrified me. Her words horrified me. The commercial ditty in my head vanished before the frightening line of a poem with which Patriarch Arsenius IV Šakabenta threatened Belgrade in the eighteenth century:

"The wild boar will devour your young."

CHAPTER 42

On the feeling of great solitude and the prediction of a new sinkhole

After I had met Irina at Zora's grave, I asked myself a question which could be called sentimental but could also be called essential: How many people are left in the world who care about me? I tried to ignore that question as soon as I asked it, but it was too late to take it back. It's not easy to look at the sun with open eyes. Or at death. Or at one's own life.

The Millennium countdown still continued. In the year 1998 nothing happened. Only the Hegelian Absolute Spirit was moving from East to West. But seriously, I was barely aware of what was going on that year. The boring evil simply kept multiplying. With his allies the fascists, Tarquin the Proud tried to crush the University and the free press. The misery in Kosovo grew into an armed uprising of the Albanians. That almost certainly meant yet another new sinkhole. Faced with the certainty of a new war, I kept repeating to myself Zora's darkly humorous consolation:

"Life will pass."

I woke up in the middle of the night wondering how many innocent lives had been destroyed in this country. I started to weep.

My world was dissolving in evil like sugar in water. I was like that bird from New Guinea that spends its entire life walking on water lilies without ever expecting to feel firm ground underneath its feet. Everything around me was disassembled, but I lived and things happened. I couldn't understand that the sun kept shining on all of this, that I kept waking up, still able to keep on going.

In my solitude, I remembered the mime Jean Louis Barrault who took a rope to hang himself in the movie *Children of Paradise*. A girl took it away from him and started to skip rope. Then a housemaker came by and use the rope to hang her linen. Jean Louis Barrault looked into the mirror and smiled. Much to my surprise, I survived the fall of all the pillars that supported my world, but I had stayed alone. Thomas Mann taught that awareness is the same as solitude, but – was that a comforting thought?

I stayed like a newborn, like one on his deathbed.

I stayed horribly alone.

CHAPTER 43

In which New York spins around Bane like a glittering hurricane. In New York, Bane runs into my father and has an argument with him

There was an important change in my solitary life – I bought a computer and began to trade emails with Bane in New York. Srđan Šaper from *The Idols* once said that each Belgradian ex-patriot takes a piece of his city with him, so we can eventually communicate with those fragments scattered all over the world. And he was right.

I confidentially informed one of those scattered fragments that I had gone out to dinner with a few women but there was no chemistry. Those "romantic encounters" – I wrote to my dear friend Bane – were bottomless pits of boredom. As long as my dentist gave me a shot of novocaine, I'd rather go to see him than spend another evening like that again.

In my next email I informed Bane that I grew close to my grandpa Teofil as he entered his old age. Teofil Đorđević once believed that people grow old because of their carelessness or because of some wrongdoing. Old age has now caught up with him. Teofil's lips looked mummified and his nose fossilized. (Dear Bane, am I going to wind up like that one day?) He bought an Irish setter called Žika, whom he loved a lot and walked regularly. Coming back from his evening walks, Teofil clinked his medicine bottles and hummed: "In their white attires, doctors look like vampires."

"As you age, the essence of who you are shrinks as your troubles expand," my grandpa told me. "And who can tell the difference between the two anyway?"

I wrote to Bane that the situation in Belgrade wasn't calming down. It was like some hellish pit was bubbling beneath us. Geographically, the city remained in the same location, but it seemed to me it was moving farther and farther away. Buildings were sinking. The fault lines underneath the city kept shifting incrementally. The TV continued to bring idiots into my apartment. I spent a lot of time following what these idiots were up to – what some bloodsucking monster accomplished or what some werewolf stated publicly. I lived on an emotional rollercoaster. At times, it seemed that my city was full of enormous energy. At other times, it seemed that spite and envy provided the only social cohesion in it, much like among the tribesmen from Doba Island in East New Guinea, which Ruth Benedict wrote about. I concluded with these words:

"You believe that you'd be an equally good person anywhere in the world. You're wrong. If you lived here, you'd be a drunk."

Despite the sharp words I directed towards my Belgrade, Bane's fascination with New York got under my skin. Bane couldn't describe New York with more enthusiasm even if he had wanted to sell it to me. He wrote that on the subway platforms someone was always playing music – something was always going on. Bane soaked in the energy that the streets of New York radiated. He could never get enough of that city. In the morning, he watched the rosy fingers of dawn touch the just awakened faces of Latinos. In the afternoon, he watched the eyelids of tired people on the subway gently fall.

For Bane, New York was the city in which all the cultures of the world intermingled. In that universal place, Mexican skeletons yodeled to the glory of the Amida Buddha. Cubans laughed through their trumpets as they played Sumerian music composed in Uruk in the third millennium before the Common Era. But New York also looked like Marseille gone wild: every second woman in the street had a Mediterranean face like our Zora.

Bane confessed to me that he took regular walks through Central Park with our invisible Zora. Zora was the only person who immigrated to America after she died. Such an immigrant wouldn't exist in the Ellis Island registry. Bane related how the two of them ambled along the inner spiral of the Guggenheim or spent afternoons in ancient Egypt which is located in the glass wing of the Metropolitan. Living Bane and dead Zora pressed their foreheads against the black glass panes on the top floor of the World Trade Center as they observed the city. The streets were gold. The city lights were stars. Bane and Zora became dizzy when they climbed the double stairs to the roof of the city's tallest building. It felt like the building would collapse at that very moment. They quieted their upset stomachs and took a look at the Hudson, the East River, New Jersey, and Queens from the roof. They locked their eyes on Brooklyn where Bane lived in a building which used to be a Romanian synagogue. Next to him, there lived a Puerto Rican who kept his roosters for cock fights on the fire escape. That wasn't the most beautiful apartment in the world, but Bane liked it. In general, Bane liked the shining city in which he lived.

"A strange city. A good city," he used to tell the lady who ran the Greek restaurant where he worked.

"This city is normal," Polimnia Papas responded. "All other cities are strange."

The restaurant *Delphi* where Bane worked was located at the corner of Eighth Avenue and Forty Sixth Street. The owner was Sotiris Papas, a Greek from Alexandria. Sotiris was too old, so his fat daughter Polimnia managed the restaurant. The good woman's name was the abbreviated version of the name of the

Muse of Sacred Poetry, Polyhymnia. At first, waiting tables seemed very romantic to Bane. He enjoyed lighting flames underneath silver cupolas that kept the food warm. When he filled a bucket with ice cubes, it appeared to be full of diamonds. He imagined himself as Hermes or Felix Krull in the restaurant.

Bane looked good in his white shirt and tie. Unnervingly polite, he approached tables and took orders. He returned quickly and placed lamb sausages or octopus salad before the guests. He learned how to pour wine sliding his fingers into the punt. He calculated tips in a fraction of a second. He draped tables with the grace of a matador. He learned to steal and quickly devour sweets, not backing down to the gluttonous lackey from Mozart's opera. Polimnia Papas tolerated his appetite and even his occasional tardiness. The only forbidden thing at *Delphi*, the one that would get you fired, was fighting with the customers.

So Bane had a fight with a customer.

The customer was my father Andrija Đorđević. During a visit to New York, Andrija's gallerist took him to *Delphi*. A Serbian from France and a couple of Russians from Brighton Beach were also with him. Already a bit tipsy, they came to eat. Andrija ordered spanakopita and a bottle of *retsina*. Bane poured him his wine with ominous kindness. Then he removed his waiter's mask and asked:

"Are you Andrija Đorđević?"

"Yes."

"I'm your son's friend."

"Ahaaaa!" Andrija shouted so that the people at the next table turned around. The painter pushed his chair away and got up. He called the matron. He informed her that the waiter was his son's friend and insisted that Bane join them and have a drink. Without waiting for her reply, Andrija made a threat:

"If this young man doesn't join us, we'll all leave."

"Of course. He can join you," the fat Muse Polimnia promptly responded. She acquiesced partly due to her good nature and partly due to her desire to keep the customers who ordered a new bottle of wine every five minutes. In his waiter's shirt and bow tie, Bane sat at their table and the party continued to drink.

"How's Belgrade?" Andrija asked him.

Bane coughed and answered:

"Tarquin the Proud introduced the elements of medieval culture into Serbian life. He privatized the public domain. Anecdotes became more important than abstract rules and rhetoric more important than logic. The importance of religion increased. Bands of thieves introduced the concept of war economy. The principle 'a single tyrant is better than many tyrants' regained importance."

„You don't say," mumbled Andrija Đorđević.

"I'm afraid our country has suffered a more severe socio-cultural regression in the last ten years than any other country in the twentieth century," Bane concluded.

"You don't say," this time my father answered with open hostility. "The Parisian Serbs tell me something quite different. They tell me that you can get anything in Belgrade and people live very normal lives."

"Do you want to know what your son has to say about it?" Bane cut him short. "He insists that I would've certainly become a drunk had I stayed in Belgrade."

In his youth, Andrija Đorđević was strange, wild, and one of a kind as if he was an alien from a different planet. Much to Bane's disappointment, he was now reduced to a clichéd version of a nationalist who, more or less intelligently, repeated slogans pushed by the media. Some of his insights were interesting but some were completely outlandish, and he went back and forth without any transition whatsoever. Bane couldn't believe what he heard when

Andrija told him that he was fond of Tarquin the Proud. Soon – as is the case among emigres – Bane engaged in a shouting match with my father and his friend. The Serb from France appeared to be a capital example of expatriotic madness. His hard-headedness looked to Bane like the locked jaws of a bull terrier. Yelling, he said how Albanians settled the sacred Serbian land in order to trade in heroin and have a dozen kids each.

"First, just like us, they have mothers too," Bane replied with boredom. "Second, a skinny peace is better than a fat conflict."

"You're clueless," Andrija shot him down scornfully.

"No, *you* are clueless."

Bane was drinking ever more fiercely with the painters while Polimnia Papas served them. Amazed, Polimnia counted the bottles of *retsina* she had brought to the table.

"Why are you drinking this shit?" Bane yelled and first ordered a bottle of *demestica*, than *danielis*, and finally some expensive wine from Cyprus.

The more they drank, the less polite the tone of their conversation turned. They not only fought about politics but everything else as well. That was half conversation, half delirious ranting... A pathetic conversation among expatriots... As the expatriots argued, New York spun around them like a glittering hurricane. Neon signs glowed above deli shops. Aided by their lights, a black homeless woman was reading a Spanish-English dictionary as she sat on her bags. Yellow cabs honked. People rushed along the streets. A Russian painter said that the diversity of New York reminded him of Constantinople. Bane and my father's friends talked and shouted and argued. Bane not only didn't lose his job over this fracas – the Muse Polimnia and the centenarian Sotiris Papas joined them at the table just before the restaurant closed. Polimnija showed Andrija a picture of her daughter who was studying medicine.

"No one must humiliate Serbia," Andrija Đorđević shouted and expressed his fear of the global spread of Islam. Polimnia and the centenarian Sotiris Papas backed him without hesitation. With his bruised, ancient voice, Sotiris complained that Turks in America are much more influential than Greeks.

"Why is that?" Andrija asked.

In response, Sotiris rolled his eyes like St. Sebastian. The Serb from France despaired because the Serbian medieval monasteries weren't included in the exhibition *The Glory of Byzantium* at the Metropolitan. The misunderstood members of the Byzantine Commonwealth traded furious hand gestures, knowingly raised eyebrows, and eloquent shrugs. In *Delphi*, they prophesized that Islam would spread all over the world. Bane knew that the Italian pseudoscience that insisted that nothing is what it seems is called *dietrology*. It turned out that Andrija Đorđević, Sotiris Papas, Polimnia, and even my father's American gallerist were all dietrologists. All except Bane agreed that invisible puppeteers pulled the strings of global politics and that the world fell victim to a big conspiracy. The albino gallerist outshined everyone as he insisted that people never went to the Moon and that Armstrong's joyful bouncing over the lunar surface was but a fabrication used to score a point in the Cold War...

"Nothing in the world is scarcer than a clear plan," Bane countered quoting Napoleon.

"Even a paranoid has enemies," the gallerist responded quoting Delmore Schwartz.

After they emptied another bottle, my father started to interrogate Bane about me. He asked him what kind of man I was and the way I lived. Completely drunk, Bane reproached him for spending so little time with me. Andrija looked him in the eye and said:

"First, my own way of life has hardly prepared me for being a good father. Second," Andrija changed the expression on his face,

"I have my own goal and, in order to reach it, I would walk across the dead bodies of my children."

"That's not an excuse," Bane waved him off.

Andrija didn't agree about anything with my friend, but he liked his brashness. At the end of the evening, he embraced him and said:

"The place of our birth, Belgrade, is an open wound. As soon as it scabs over, dirty nails rip the scab off. Through centuries, it was impossible to live in that place – one could escape only to go back. I left Belgrade due to one evil. In the next generation, another evil chased you away. If we could live in a normal world, you and I would be friends in Belgrade."

At these words, Bane raised a finger and responded in a drunken murmur:

"The problem is that currently rational thinking is prohibited in our country. You know, your ass can be right or your dick can be right, but most of the time it's your head that's right."

Andrija cracked up, embraced, and kissed Bane. The door opened and the river of tobacco smoke poured out into the street. It took a while for them to say goodbye. The effeminate gallerist gave Bane his phone number.

"Next time you come to New York, come to *Delphi*. Dinner will be on us," Polimnia shouted after Andrija Đorđević.

As he stumbled along Forty-sixth Street, the building fractured into Cubist shapes before Bane. Colors mixed and swirled in his eyes. All the sounds of the city curved into a snail's shell and settled in his ears. Like a guardian angel, the invisible Zora repeatedly saved him from oncoming cars. Finally, drunken Bane waved down an Indian cab driver and gave him his Brooklyn address. He sat back in the comfortable seat and, before dozing off, he sighed:

"Life is so strange!"

CHAPTER 44

In which Bane warns me of the bombs which are about to fall on my head

As soon as I finished washing my face in the morning, I rushed to peer into the virtual abyss of my computer screen. Undressed, I went to make a cup of coffee and stole a glance at the mirror. The lock of hair from my childhood pictures still curled in the middle of my forehead, but the hair on both sides had grown thinner. The skin under my eyes was now crumpled. I sat down at my computer in my undershirt and for a while with great interest stared at the fluorescent urine smudge on my underwear. Then, with my first cup of coffee, I opened my email, read Bane's messages, and responded. We talked about all sorts of things, whatever came to mind. I informed Bane that public buses with missing sections of the floor and no lights at night became the norm in Belgrade. I confessed to my old friend that I envied him. Bane responded that moving to another country was the same as being the main character in *Heart of Darkness*. That's a no win situation. I responded that only those who never tried to win have a reason to feel sorry.

Bane wrote that – when he was not working at the restaurant – he was taking computer programing classes at Columbia. He insisted that he was ready to develop the marketing project for *Macintosh* for eastern Serbia. The computer would be advertized as a handy planner for death anniversaries and funereal customs. In the Timok region, *Macintosh* would be sold with instructions on "how to protect your software from the evil eye." Bane predicted that one day people would click the mouse a few times and view the dreams of any historical figure. He also predicted that on the computer we would soon be able to read the thoughts of angels. The angels would reveal to us what we could expect from the coming Millennium.

This is what the angels would tell us:

"When the Millennium arrives, there will be paradise on earth, the coming of the Kingdom of God and (for our parents) Communism. To start with, every person will have a white cat. People will walk the streets with white cats. The dead will come to life and we'll have time to have long conversations with those with whom we didn't have time to have long conversations in life. We will ask questions that have never been answered. We will apologize to those whom we wronged, and those who wronged us will apologize to us. Time will not unfold in a linear manner – everything will happen simultaniously. That way, we will have time to repeatedly revisit the most beautiful moments of our lives. In a sense, each man will be many men. Seasons will exist at the same time. A winter day, a summer day, and a day of golden autumn which is like a slice of an aromatic canteloupe will follow in succession. And the icing on the cake will be whimsical spring with the wind scattering butterflies all over the vista and all things emitting fragrances. I hope I'll have an oportunity to learn a few languages and several crafts. I'll master the craft of cooking. I'll practice *tai-che*," wrote Bane. "That will be a second life and also – all lives..."

Then my funny friend dropped this pompous tone and admitted that New York hadn't changed him, so he was still wasting his time staring at cleavages and low cut dresses. What impressed him the most at Columbia University – where Mihajlo Pupin once taught – Bane condensed in a single email with the subject-matter line:

A description of an ass

"She has shapely thighs and a narrow waist. She likes to put her hands on her hips as she talks. Her ass is – charming... It's nicely formed and bigger than fashion designers would deem desirable. Those powerful hemispheres look particularly interesting in profile. She has a black woman's ass although she's white and a blond. Today she's wearing purple pants. She's writing on the board and her waist is beautifully accentuated. As she writes, her ass trembles slightly, and I'm observing it with teary eyes like a Romantic listening to Chopin. Even though she's turned towards the board, she puts her hands on her hips and steps aside, crossing her legs. Has she practiced this move? Her panty lines are discernable though vaguely... but, yes, I can see them. The parts of the hemispheres that aren't covered with panties are particularly interesting. God, what color are those panties? Whatever color they are, I'd love to shred them with my teeth. She's now talking about 'fuzzy logic.' She's my professor of 'Scientific Programming in C' and her name is Jen Martinson."

I noticed that Bane wrote to me about personal things while I wrote to him about history and the so-called politics. To his jovial letters I responded with my gloomy emails in which I didn't try to conceal my belief that the situation in Kosovo, in the rump Yugoslavia, and in Belgrade, will develop for the worse. My prediction was that things would head not only in the worst but in the most stupid direction. The logic which preferred a bloody defeat to any kind of settlement ruled over Serbia. And this is because – I wrote to Bane – this ruffian logic considers the very idea of compromise as a total defeat. I moaned about how my people had been in a decade-long love affair with a jackass, like Titania in *Midsummer Night's Dream*. I was waiting for the effects of weed to wind down. In the meantime, I foresaw a bloodbath in Kosovo and saw in advance bombs falling on Belgrade.

Bane wrote back to tell me that I had turned into a bigger paranoid than my father. He wrote that good and bad governments would come and go while female asses would keep captivating men for all time. Men will crave women and women will crave men and that's how it will be for ever and ever until the end of time, amen. It was obvious that Bane was trying to pry me away from my ugly state of mind. He wrote in *post script*:

"Let's drop these heavy topics, my dear Milan. How's your life?"

"I'm reading German Expressionist poetry and pretending that everything is normal," I wrote back. "What else can I do?"

I refused to engage in small talk with Bane. I was surprised that he expected me to ignore what my life depended on. At the beginning of the breakup of Yugoslavia in 1991, I still hoped that we could somehow hit the brakes, wake up to reality, or miss the wall we were rushing into. Now, at the beginning of 1999, I didn't hope for any kind of miracle. Tired from living in an endless tunnel, I anticipated another war. My emotional rollercoaster switched into the self-loathing mode. I started raving against my own people.

"I don't believe in racism," I wrote in my next email. "But we seem to be genetically impaired. I can't wait for us to die out, so some other people can come to work and live here. It's a pity to let such a beautiful country go to waste!"

"That's not you talking, it's your despair!" Bane responded. "Self-loathing is as disgusting as any other form of racism. Talking about our so-called motherland, the distance from which I currently observe it gives it a quality I wasn't able to see from up close. You know where biblical hell is located? On the Sun! It's the distance that makes the Sun the source of life."

It's clear why I spent so much time before the computer, communicating with Bane – I was the loneliest man in the world. But why did Bane waste his time corresponding with me? Obviously, Bane felt lonely too. The computer screen provided a virtual parlor for the interaction between two solitudes, one in New York and one in Belgrade.

Sometimes our correspondence looked less like a dialogue and more like two monologues that ran side by side. I resembled one of those irritating eccentrics who are unable to give up their obsessive topics. C'mon, man, give me a break from politics, Bane used to tell me. But I couldn't do it. I kept talking about evil and anticipated evil to happen. I wrote to him that each week a dozen policemen were killed in Kosovo. A decade-long rule of a disastrous government and two confronting nationalisms were leading to a war in which Yugoslavia would have to face NATO. I wrote to Bane about a brainy Serbian general who declared that he didn't see a reason why Yugoslavia wouldn't defeat the nineteen countries of the NATO alliance. That general and his puppeteer Tarquin the Proud appeared to me as people who were perched on the seventh floor deliberating whether to jump. Well-meaning bystanders told them: If you jump, you may either die or get crippled. The two men didn't believe them – they seemed more inclined to find it out for themselves.

And so they did.

Finally, even Bane realized that I wasn't as paranoid as he thought. On Tuesday, March 23rd, he woke me with a warning phone call:

"Be careful! Today or tomorrow they'll probably start bombing you."

"Thank you!" I said in a dead voice and hung up.

That day I finally opened an old email in which Bane told me how excited America was in anticipation of the Millennium. At the post office where he used to buy stamps there was a digital clock that obsessively counted down days, hours, minutes, and seconds that separated us from the Millennium. Bane sent me the millennial ad for Universal Studio's Escape theme park, published in *People* magazine. The ad claimed:

In the summer of 1999,
The theory of evolution will be written anew
The natural laws will be violated
The definition of matter will be changed permanently
The limitations of gravity will be cancelled
And time will not flow only in one direction.
The only question is:
ARE YOU READY?

CHAPTER 45

In which Bojan and I look at the millennial sky

When the bombs started to fall on my head, my first reaction wasn't fear but disbelief. The siren that announced each attack sounded like Zeus who had just abducted Europa and, transformed into a giant bull, bellowed deliriously over Belgrade. On the first day, the bellowing sounded funny, but later it became terrifying. The atmosphere in the city was truly millennial. People climbed up to the roofs of buildings and watched the circle of fire around the city. Tomahawk missiles looked like meteors. Whenever they hit their targets somewhere in Batajnica, my apartment complex would hover for a moment in the air before settling down into place. At times it seemed like the explosions took out the ground from under my feet and hurled me and my building some thirty miles away. I felt as if I was thrown out of my body. Was my building intact or was it not? Was I still there or was I not? The red glare of the anti-aircraft defense from the ground harmonized with the missiles in the sky. The sky looked like huge fireworks, but my blood turned into ice at the thought of what it would deliver to someone – or to me.

In the shelter which, in our case, was an ordinary basement, I was reading a book of German Expressionist poetry. The woman sitting across from me was a Serbian refugee from Croatia. One of her breasts had just been surgically removed. The night after she had left the hospital she spent in the basement. I watched her cry. Albanian women cried throughout Kosovo. My mother cried whenever I called her on the phone. I asked myself whether there was a scale to weigh tears, determining which ones were heavy and which ones were light, which ones were righteous and which ones were profane, which ones could be ignored and which ones couldn't. Instead of racking my brain with such thoughts, I buried my nose into the book of German Expressionist poetry. While a red column of flame rose up from the outskirts of Belgrade, in my basement I was reading a poem by Jakob von Hoddis:

End of the World

From pointy noggins, townies' hats fly,
The air is full of ear-wrenching screams,
Roofers shake and tumble from the beams,
On the beach – they say – the tide grows high.

The tempest arrives and levies are shot,
The sea runs wild submerging the ridges.
Most people have noses dripping with snot
Railway trains are falling off the bridges.

When I finished reading the last line, a distant blast shook the building. First I gaped. Then I dropped the book with the millennial poem. I realized how small I was. I realized I couldn't do anything. In my insignificance, I felt humbleness forced on me – a Christian experience, if you will. I felt the presence of God. But unlike Boris, who felt the presence of God in the bombs falling on Sarajevo, I felt the presence of God in the bombs falling on Belgrade.

Throughout the night, the siren bellowed and the terrifying fireworks blossomed in the sky. Throughout the day, catkins flew above the Danube and everything looked normal. On one such "normal" day in the second week of the bombardment, someone knocked on my door. I couldn't believe my eyes when I saw Irina at the threshold. With one hand, Irina held a suitcase and with the other she dragged along a four-year-old boy, his face deadly serious.

I held out my hand: "Hi!"

"You have a cigarette in your hand," she noticed.

Entering the room, we were both stiff. We sat down. The room was dark in the middle of the day, and I flipped the switch. The chandelier became rejuvenated with light. I noticed that my visitor had bags under her eyes and that she was very agitated.

Irina sat on the edge of the couch. She bit her lip. She looked at me sideways. She spoke incoherently. She told me that she and her son Bojan were hiding in Boris' parents' house in Hicktown for a while. (Thank God that house had been finally used for something.) Irina repeatedly said that she worried about Bojan's safety. I knew that Boris and Dada killed the younger Vukotić and his pregnant wife. Irina reminded me that Vukotić's wife's father, the Sinister Dude, vowed to hit Boris's family in retalliation. When Irina's father Čedomir moved to Moscow where he had a trading company, she didn't dare go with him. I was about to ask myself why she was telling me all that, when she looked me in the eye and asked:

"May I leave Bojan with you? Please, Milan. No one knows about you."

"Careful!" I thought. The whole thing seemed crazy. Irina's father Čedomir was neither naïve nor helpless. He even had access to Tarquin the Proud himself. He could've hired ten bodyguards to escort Bojan to the plane. I knew that there were snipers and that the kid could be killed at the airport or in Moscow. However, something was off kilter big time here. I stared at Irina inquisitively: Was she truly terrified? Or was she on heroin? Or had she – God forgive me – gone insane and that was why she wanted to leave the kid with me.

Irina took me by the hand and repeated:

"No one knows about you."

Then my former love began to cry with a screeching sound of glass being cut. I tried to remember her when she was carefree. I tried to remember how fond I was of her. When I failed, I realized that a half of my life had ended irrevocably. The female face before me shattered like a dropped plate. Irina cried with her horrible, screeching sound. Frozen, little Bojan watched his mother cry. Then his lips trembled as well.

"Enough! I'll do it. I'll do anything, just stop crying."

The words came out despite myself and completely terrified me. The late Zora often wondered: Should we pity evil fools as well? She believed we should. Everyone always takes it out on the innocent and thus evil never ends, I thought. If Irina was insane, this kid wasn't. He needed help.

"Thank you, thank you," Irina said and laughed as if she was sucking a lemon.

"He's a good man," she told Bojan. "Love him and listen to him. Mommy will be back soon."

She thrust the suitcase with Bojan's things on me.

"Only until this is over."

Only until this is over? I wrote down Čedomir's phone number in Moscow and Boris' in Thessaloniki hoping one of them would be more reasonable than Irina.

Our flimsy hug looked like a hug of two astronauts in space. Irina's tears smeared her makeup as she was closing the door. With his frozen face, the four-year-old Bojan stared after his mother. At that moment, Irina's face was a printed page. The page read: "All is lost!"

"Thank you," she called from the door. "I love you."

Never before had she told me that she loved me. I bit my lip because yet another of my life's desires was fulfilled as a farce.

Irina left while I stayed behind to lightly drum my fingers on my brow as if playing the piano: What am I going to do now? I stayed behind in the city under bombardment to take care of a kid someone wanted to murder in revenge. My unsuspected bravery frightened me so much I wanted to slap myself on the face. Why didn't I tell Irina: Sorry, but what you're saying is completely insane. Why didn't I tell her that every mother must take care of her own kid? Why didn't I drive her away? Boris always flaunted his courage. I had always been Hamlet. How come in the end I was supposed to protect his son from vendetta? They could kill both me and Grandpa together with little Bojan. Now I couldn't do anything anymore. I could only hope those thugs really were clueless about my existence. I could only pray to God that, in a city under bombardment, the assassins would have other fish to fry.

In the following days, I did everything I could to make friends with Bojan. I told him I grew up with his mom and dad. I promised him that Mom and Dad would be back soon and that we would call them on the phone. In the meantime, I called Irina's place in Neimar and dialed the numbers in Thessaloniki and Moscow. No one ever responded. I didn't know how to talk with such a small kid, so I asked him:

"What's more fun – peeing or pooping?"

"I don't know," the sharp Bojan responded. "Nothing is fun."

That was when he first smiled at me. I kissed him on the head and took him to introduce him to Grandpa Teofil. We found Teofil in his room clinking his medicine bottles and humming the silly song: "I went to the pharmacy today, they want to cut my ass, they say…" I cleared my throat, put my hand on Bojan's shoulder, and said that the kid would stay with us for the time being. The old Surrealist wasn't surprised to find that a strange boy showed up in the apartment. He was constantly surprised by one thing only: How come he, Teofil Đorđević, dwelt in this world at all?

Grandpa's Irish setter Žika barked at the small kid, and the boy burst into tears. Teofil pretended to hit the dog, wiped away Bojan's tears, and sat him on his lap.

"What would you like to be when you grow up?" he asked the boy to calm him down.

Bojan understood but didn't answer.

"Never mind," Teofil smiled with a smile of a turtle. "I haven't decided what I want to be when I grow up either."

Not until we were back in my room, did the boy press his lips against my ear and confessed:

"I'd like to be a king."

The strange life we lived looked normal during the day. It was spring. I've already mentioned that catkins flew above the river. I've forgotten to say that young men regularly went out to cafes and checked out girls. One could almost forget there was a war going on. But each night, Zeus – turned into a giant bull – began to bellow above the city: air raid. Driven crazy by the sirens, a sensitive rhinoceros in Belgrade Zoo committed suicide by banging his head against the wall.

Because of Bojan, I reneged on my earlier decision not to go to the shelter. Each night I carried Bojan to the basement where the draught played with cobwebs. I took with me the book of German Expressionist poetry and an Angora blanket for the kid. Teofil stayed behind in the apartment. Generally speaking, he tried to ignore the war. He took his Irish setter Žika out for a walk at any time and grumbled:

"A dog goes out to take a piss when he wants to and not when NATO wants him to."

When, before dawn, the siren released me from the basement, I found Grandpa doubled over in the armchair beneath the painting called *St. George on the Dragon Killing the Horse.*

"It's over!" I thought. The golden letters of an epitaph already started to glow underneath Grandpa's slouching body: *Teofil Đorđević, born in the First Balkan War. Expired in the last year of the Millennium. Born in a war. Died in a war.*

At that moment, Teofil opend his eyes and winked:

"Interesting, huh?"

"Bite me, you old fool!" I could barely keep from saying. I went on calling Thessaloniki and Moscow but no one responded.

In the meantime, I taught Bojan how to wash his hands. Bojan turned a piece of soap between his palms and enjoyed watching the white foam gloves before he rinsed them off. The most difficult thing was to put him to bed. Whenever sirens started to howl or the building foundation shook from blasts, he didn't cry – only his eyes widened as if to swallow the whole world. I would wrap the blanket around him and talk to him soothingly. The neighbors in the shelter thought he was my son. They winked at one another whispering how the fairies took his mom.

For some time now, flames hadn't only been shooting up from the outskirts. We all looked down in shame walking by the ruins in the center of town. More and more the city resembled the one Čedomir had liberated fifty years ago. The clock tower on the Ministry of Railways Building collapsed and we all wondered: What standard time do we live by now? Bombs damaged the chemical plant in Pančevo. Poisonous substances spilled into the Danube. My aunt fled from the poisoned Pančevo and slept in my mother's apartment. Every day I called my mother to cheer her up. She told me that her neighbors walked around like zombies. A complete stranger in the street would lift up his head and ask:

"Where is all this going, Madam? What will happen to us?"

In the shelter I got to know better my neighbors whom I had never before said "good morning" so that they could hear the final "g." The neighbors told each other stories. They encouraged one another. They hated together. A wise man once said that it's hard to embrace democracy if it's coming to you in the shape of a bomb. They said how the granite building next to the city's maternity ward was hit. Still bleeding, new mothers rushed to the nurseries, while the doctors tried to keep them separated from their newborns so they could evacuate them orderly. The neighbors talk about cluster bombs which plowed through the downtown of Niš. They talked about a Novi Sad bicyclist who was thrown up in the air together with a bombed bridge – and survived. They talked about the people who were lighting candles on Belgrade bridges. The little girl who died on her potty in Batajnica they turned into an icon. I knew that there were war crimes in Kosovo. Other people in my basement turned a blind eye to the columns of Albanian refugees that crowded border crossings to Albania and Macedonia. I was thinking about those refugees' tears up in the cold mountains. I imagined how, somewhere on the Macedonian border, family members reunited and asked: Where are the others? Where's the uncle? What happened to the neighbors? I remembered a line from a poem that says: "Each word and each song know only its own love."

At times, Bojan would wake up for reasons which had nothing to do with the bombardment. Then it seemed that his crusty eyes didn't recognize me as he whimpered:

"When will Mommy come back?"

"She will. Mommy will come back, don't worry," I held him close while he wiped his tears with his tiny fists.

One event concerning that kid remained in my memory much clearer than any other event from the war. The infernal fireworks ornamented the sky above Belgrade. I was lying next to the sleeping Bojan, engrossed in Georg Heym's lines from *German Expressionist Poetry*. When I turned over, Bojan wasn't in the shelter. He simply wasn't there. The blanket that I wrapped around him was unwrapped. I threw my jacket over my shoulders and dashed out into the street. I took a step to the left and then to the right. Where was he? Two thoughts ran through my head: "If I could only find him," and "I'll skin him alive once I catch him."

With a sudden sense of certainty, I ran towards Kosančićev Venac.

I spotted Bojan across the road from Mika Alas' house. I wanted to grab him and drag him back into the shelter. However, something in the boy's bearing stopped me. The child stood with his head thrown back, completely fascinated. He looked at the Belgrade sky lit by Tomahawks and the shimmer of anti-aircraft fire. With clenched fists and wide opened eyes, he stared at the celestial omens. It looked as if Bojan, his mouth open, was waiting for a comet like a fire eater waiting for his torch. As I observed that four-year-old child, the last lines from Georg Heym's poem "The Suburb" which I had just finished reading, flashed through my head:

> *At the fortress gate, with a cripple's swagger,*
> *A dwarf is puffed up in his black silky coat,*
> *He lifts his eyes to the green dome*
> *Where meteors slowly carve their paths.*

CHAPTER 46

Which describes my fight with the world

Bane was living in America, and I was living in Belgrade. Because "America" bombed Belgrade, it followed that "Bane" bombed "me." During the war, email was still functional, so we continued to trade messages. However, I felt that we, as correspondents, weren't in an equitable position at all. Bane observed New York from the World Trade Center. He wrote to me from the top of the world. I responded from the sunken Atlantis where birds had turned into fish long ago. Or did I write from Dostoevsky's underground? It didn't matter.

Because everything took the worst possible turn, it didn't surprise me that Bane and I began to fight. We were both aware that in each new war someone would go crazy, but we couldn't agree which one of us went insane this time. We both lived on emotional rollercoasters which came to a halt at different levels. It was my turn now to defend Belgrade, while Bane attacked it.

On American TV, Bane Janović watched hundreds of thousands of Albanian refugees swarming on the Macedonian border. Despite her fear of the global Islamic conspiracy, his boss Polimnia Papas was deeply moved:

"Those children's eyes!" she yelled. "O my heart! O my heart! Those children's eyes!"

Bane and I shoved our heads into computer screens and argued in a virtual room in between New York and Belgrade solitudes. In a sense, that was a fight between "me" and the "world" except the "world" was embodied in the person of my old friend Bane.

The world was telling me:

"The terror in Kosovo must be stopped at any price."

I responded:

"I'd love to see those guilty of the crimes against Albanian civilians wash their bloody hands with their own tears. But I'd be more at peace if NATO's reports didn't spread the same lies I used to see as Tarquin the Proud's exclusive domain. The authors of those reports pretend that the ecological catastrophe in Pančevo doesn't exist. Officially, they're waging a war against Tarquin the Proud, who's completely safe in his bunker. He is safe, but I'm not.

In Belgrade, power outages and water shortages played a game of leapfrog. I wash my dishes by candlelight as if I'm performing a satanic ritual. Each time a siren wails, little Bojan's chin trembles. So I ask him if he's scared. He says: 'No – I'm only awfully cold.' What can I say? It's beyond me. At times, it seems to me we've been collectively labeled subhuman and any way they treat us is better than we deserve."

The "world" embodied in the person of my friend Bane asked me if I expected the West to stick to the highest legal standards dealing with someone who completely ignores even the Ten Commandments.

"Judges don't rape rapists or eat cannibals," I responded. "The difference between the judge and the criminal is in the judge's adherence to the law. If that's not the case, we deal with a criminal disguised as a judge."

The "world" asked me: "What's your problem? Wasn't it you who, during all these years, complained about the euphemistic treatment of crime and the wanton miracle of self-delusion? Has it ever occurred to you that a man doesn't reap anything other than what he sows?"

I reminded Bane of the time when he lied curled up in a military hospital. I reminded him that he was both Jonas and Daniel. I reminded him that no one in the world is waiting for me with out-stretched arms and "no-entry" is stamped at each border-cross-ing. I asked him if he believed that lecturing somebody who has bombs falling on his head is an example of ultimate tact.

"And do you think you have it worse than those in Sarajevo?" the "world" asked.

"Of course I don't," I answered. "But I think I have it worse than you who's lecturing me. On one hand, I wish the worst for those who carry out crimes against civilians. In order to tell you what I think of them, let me use a religious parable: Imagine a pile of sand as big as the universe from which one grain is taken away once in every ten thousand years. The day will come when that pile will finally disappear, but the end of sufferings of those con-demned in hell won't be any closer than it is now.

On the other hand, I think that all the hemophiliacs, thieves, old women, homosexuals, politicians, and pensioners are being punished because they still buy cigarettes in the city in which they were born. I also think that the idea of the penguin-like sameness of all the members of a certain group and their collective guilt is es-sentially a fascist idea. No one who believes that can be called anti-fascist.

I raise my hand and humbly declare that I'm an individual. I've spent a lot of time in front of a mirror in my life in order to fi-nally convince myself that I exist. I am Milan Đorđević, a Belgradian and I am lonely. I live in between Tarquin the Proud who calls me a traitor and foreign journalists who call me a fascist. The before-said journalists are Tarquin the Proud's best friends. Both sides perfectly complement each other's prejudices and, jointly, make me invisible. May I bother you with a question as to why I am invisible?"

"O, world!" I called out. "Do you ever try to step into my shoes? For years, I've been publicly hurling sharp words at

Tarquin the Proud and what's happened? Nothing! I, a critic of Tarquin the Proud, am supported by bombs which paradoxically rain on my, not his, head.

The fact that bears with their blooded jaws have been growling in my name for the last ten years doesn't mean that I don't have anything to say at all. I can't constantly throw ashes on my head if I want to keep my eyes open. And I need my eyes to see the shadow that the smoke from the hit chemical plants in Pančevo casts onto the region in which I live. I need them to see that the commander of the Kosovo Liberation Army has no compunction to commit crimes no lesser then those of Tarquin the Proud's. I need them to see hundreds of thousands of Serbian refugees in 'subhuman conditions' to whom moralists won't send a dime."

"I don't imagine what I'm writing is particularly important," I wrote to the "world." "I don't imagine that you would even hear me and that the golden rooster from heaven would join the red rooster from hell in song. I'm a historian, and I know that nothing is more malleable than the past. I know that God the master of the shell game can move his hand and make things appear in a different light. Let this missive remain a testimony of despair and uncertainty," I told the world. "Let it remain a document of human weakness, of their doubts under peripheral skies in the 'wrong' part of the world."

"O my heart! O my heart!" the world responded to me in the words of Polimnia Papas. "Things with us are reduced to condemning or supporting the crime. In which category do you think your words fit? You would at least want humankind to admit – with a tear in its eye – that you've been misunderstood. You'd want the world to pat your head and say: 'Poor thing!'"

"I'm not a poor thing," I responded. "Even when I'm on my deathbed, I won't call myself a poor thing."

The conflict between Bane and me was even harsher because both of us were trying to dampen our own doubts which weakened our positions. That's why we quarreled so fiercely.

"Are you lonesome?" Bane asked me in the middle of our fight.

"My solitude is so deep that even I'm absent from it," I answered.

Despite Bane's enthusiasm in playing the role of the "world," I could still feel a sense of growing fatigue emanating from his messages. The constant smile of a waiter was wearing out his face. He set and cleared the tables in the restaurant *Delphi* too many times and so his job lost its romantic aura. Bane didn't imagine himself to be Hermes or Felix Krull anymore. In his dreams, he saw jangling rivers of forks and pyramids of glasses. After midnight, in the empty window of the restaurant, he felt like he was in an Edward Hopper painting.

Noticing the fatigue weighing Bane down, I asked him if he still loved New York in the same way.

"I am New York," Bane responded.

I dropped my head between my shoulders and asked myself if I could also say: "I am Belgrade." I realized that I couldn't run away from what I was. I slowly raised my head and concluded:

"Yes. I am Belgrade."

CHAPTER 47

A lament for Belgrade which I refused to write down because I refused to abandon my own life for an epic

I am Belgrade.

It's war once again.

A common Balkan legend tells about a specific place that wouldn't allow a city to be built on it. That legend is about me. Once again my buildings are dying a violent death.

Think where the ruins of my Roman forum are, the remnants of my public baths, of the buildings heated with steam... Where's the mighty tower of Constantine the Great from the Roman period? Where's the bishopric palace which Justinian rebuilt? Where are Despot Stefan Lazarević's numerous structures that made me look so "markedly variegated"?

Where are my houses and castles from various centuries? Where's the tower of the Byzantine *strategos*? Where's Despot Stefan Lazarević's castle which – with its four turrets – resembled "the actual home of King David"? Where are the mansions of the two Jakšić brothers erected next to the Ružica Church? Where's the Belgrade residence of Ulrich of Celje? Where are the defensive structures built on galleys that protected the city at the waterfront? Where are the Mill Tower, the Šahin Tower, the Karamustafa Tower, the Clock Tower?

Where are my gates? Where's the Clock Gate, the Rospi Gate, the Sava Gate, the Sugate, the Dungeon Gate? Where did they go, what was built from their remnants?

Where are my churches that the Turks demolished in order to use their stones to build their mosques? Where's the great cathedral metropolitan church that the Serbian King Dragutin erected in order to house the icon of the Mother of God, painted by the hand of Apostle Luke? Where are the Franciscan church in Lower Belgrade and the Church of St. Magdalene beyond the city walls? Where are the Temple of St. Archangel Michael and the Church of the Ascension of the Mother of God? Where are those three Christian churches the Turks pulled down in order to use their stones to build Mehmed Pasha Sokoli's caravan saray that "looked like a cathedral"? Where's that caravan saray now?

Where are my mosques that Germans, Hungarians, and Serbs destroyed to build their churches from their stones? Where's Suleiman the Magnificent's one hundred and fifty step tall mosque that the great Sinan built from stone he cut like wood, the interior of which was "harmonious and cozy like a mirror"? Where are the Ibrahim-bey Mosque, the Imaret Mosque, the Bairam-bey Mosque, the Haji Mehmed Mosque, the Durgut Pasha Mosque, the Halil Effendi Mosque? Where's the Sultan's Palace built in the midst of the "water town"? Where's the Grand Vizier's Palace? Where are the twenty sleeping inns, the ten bald Turkish baths, the twenty-seven singing fountains from the time when Belgrade was Baghdad?

Where is the city shown in the prints from the Baroque Wars, in which cannon balls jump like fleas? What has been left of the Italian Cornaro's fortifications from the end of the seventeenth century and the Swiss Nikola de Morez Doksat's fortifications from the early eighteenth century? Where's the promenade, lined with two-story eighteenth century buildings along the Danube from the Austrian Belgrade? Where are the churches and the monastery that used to sit on today's Student Square? Where are the Jesuit monastery and school, and the city infirmary dedicated to St. John? Where's the cathedral? Where's the Prince's Palace in Dorćol? Where are the streets that were once called Transylvania

Street, Merchant Street, Fishermen Street... They are all gone, gone in time like a tear in the rain.

I only look like a firm, white city. And yet, I'm a city made of beeswax and the invisible flame of time has been licking and melting me since the beginning. In me, for centuries, Catholics converted back to Orthodoxy and Orthodox to Catholicism "the way trodden grass springs back." Some Belgradians used the stones of my churches as building materials for mosques. Other Belgradians used the stones of my mosques to build churches. Some wise men claim that it's not good because "one can't drive a split stake into the ground." Other wise men claim that it's good because gods live between the worlds.

Have you seen fast forwarded video clips that show the blossoming and wilting of a flower in a few seconds? Imagine one such clip showing the changes of Belgrade. Imagine being able to see two thousand years of my history in twenty minutes. In that video, the flame consumes roofs and the wind plays city towers like Pan flutes. In that video, the sword cuts family trees and wars wipe out everything that has been accomplished. In that video, buildings grow and wilt like flowers. In that video, I, Belgrade, show churches and mosques only to pull them back into the earth the next moment, like a snail stretching out its horns and pulling them back again.

EPILOGUE

When I dreamed of it again, it felt like I finally surfaced after many long years and caught a breath of air.

I dreamed of a city.

I dreamed of temples and palaces. I dreamed of theaters surrounding the square where poets recited verses. I dreamed of well-dressed old men and women, full of life, who were strolling through parks. Lovers were sitting on the benches and intoxicated each other with their breath. I dreamed of sculptures that dotted the squares and the facades of buildings. I dreamed of a thousand restaurants which served the food of a thousand nations. I dreamed of wine-shops organized as neatly as libraries. I dreamed of a city with two rivers that washed its worries away and left it carefree.

I dreamed of bookstores and tea-shops where a man could comfortably grow old. I dreamed of a town where it was a pleasure to experience the change of seasons. I dreamed of a place that seduced me with details and made me fall in love with the whole. I dreamed of the City.

I smiled to the city in my dream. That was a city of eternal noon, without twilight and shadows. Angels strolled through the streets, and from windows women showered them with confetti from pillow-cases. White arms waived to me from balconies. When I opened my eyes, an angel was standing above me. The angel pointed his finger at the cliff above the waters and said:

"Look!"

I looked along the angel's finger and – everything was there.

There was a city on the cliff. The walls, whiter than a cuttle-bone, gleamed in the sun. Clusters of architecture rose on top of each other in charming disarray. Angels waved from the city walls. I recognized Simha Koen, Jehuda Lerma, Despot Stefan Lazarević, St. Sava, Nurulah Muniri Belgradi, the angel with spectacles, Dositej Obradović, Vladislav Petković Dis. Transformed, the protagonists of this book gave a bow as if after a theatrical performance. A face with Bojan's shy smile stood out among the others. My eyes tired from recognizing the faces. In my dream, countless people whose faces I couldn't see waved to me from the Belgrade city walls. I had an inkling they were Herulis, Gepids, Avars, Byzantines, Pechenegs, Huns, Hungarians, Bulgarians, Romans, Celts, Germans, Tsintsars, Armenians, Turks, and Serbs. Something happened to my mind, so I didn't know whether those who waved were dead or not yet born.

With horror in my eyes, I drank in my dream-come-true. I was shocked by its coming true. Now that my dream has come true, I could burst like a soap bubble. I felt too small to accept responsibility for my dream. I wanted to turn down the offer to play a role in the Sisyphus-like, sacred task of Founding a City. I wanted to shriek. I wanted to scream. I wanted to hide my head under my wing. I wanted to scoff at what I most wanted.

I bit my lip and cautioned myself: Be brave! Hadn't you stood a million times before a mirror preparing to take yourself seriously and settle down in your dream? On my mushy legs, I took the first step towards Belgrade, then the second, then the third. "Is this the end of having no home?" I muttered in a language I didn't know. My own language! Now I knew I wouldn't turn my back on my dream. Angels won't scream after me from the ramparts of chalk. Like a blind man, I felt the gate of Belgrade. My stomach was full of butterflies, and my fingers danced from excitement. Will my dream finally become my home in the new Millennium?

NOTE ON THE AUTHOR

Vladimir Pištalo (1960) is one of the most significant contemporary Serbian writers. His most well-known works include the books of poems in prose *Slikovnica* (Picture Book, 1981), *Manifesti* (Manifestoes,1986), *Noći* (Nights, 1986), and *Kraj veka* (End of a Century, 1999); the collections of short stories *Vitraž u sećanju* (Stain Glass in the Memory, 1996) and *Priče iz celog sveta* (Stories from all around the World, 1998); and novels *Milenijum u Beogradu* (Millennium in Belgrade, 2001), *Tesla, portret među maskama* (Tesla: A Portrait with Masks, 2008, NIN Book of the Year Award*)*, *Venecija* (Venice, 2011), and *Sunce ovog dana: Pismo Andriću* (The Sun of This Day: Letters to Andrić, 2017).

Pištalo is also the author of two unusual literary biographies: *Aleksandrida*, a fairytale-like story dealing with the life of Alexander the Great, and *Korto Maltese*.

Tesla: A Portrait with Masks was translated into sixteen languages, and *Millennium in Belgrade* into six.

Table of Contents